REVIEWS OF *THE RIVER BETWEEN US*

"Against the backdrop of the two ferocious First and Second Indo-China Wars, *The River Between Us* brought readers to a village in Central Vietnam where the entwined lives and very special friendship shared between Minh and Mai encapsulated the resilient and compassionate spirit of the Vietnamese families. Wasilewski demonstrates a thoughtful observation to a complex spectrum of both Vietnamese culture and human emotions. Following the footsteps of these two women and their families and neighbors, from the prewar Mid-Autumn procession around an old tamarind tree to the postwar harvest festival with water-puppet stage, readers will gain a close-up and heartfelt understanding of how closely the wars were to and how deeply they wounded these Vietnamese villagers, who navigated through the darkest wartime by the fiercest love and compassion for one another, and a shared hope and commitment for a quiet, enduring peace."

> \- Uyen H. "Carie" Nguyen, Texas Tech University

"Sometimes fiction is the perfect way to capture the density and complexity of history. So it is with *The River Between Us*, a masterful story that brings the traumas of the Vietnam War into sharp focus. Stephen Wasilewski deserves enormous credit for reading deeply into the history of the war and bringing that history to life through his extraordinary characters."

> \- Mark Atwood Lawrence, University of Texas at Austin
> author of *The Vietnam War: A Concise International History*

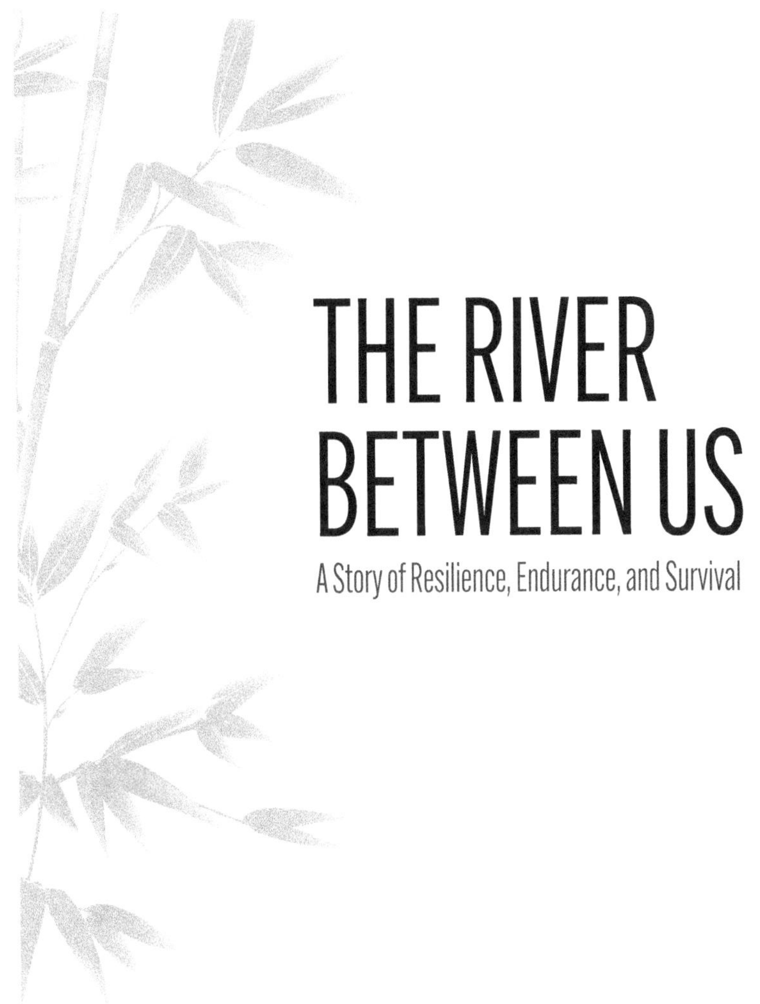

THE RIVER BETWEEN US

A Story of Resilience, Endurance, and Survival

STEPHEN WASILEWSKI

The River Between Us
by Stephen Wasilewski

Copyright © 2026
All rights reserved.
Published by Masthof Press

All rights reserved. Reproduction or utilization of this work in any form, by any means now known or herein after invented, including but not limited to xerography, photocopying and recording, and in any storage and retrieval system, is forbidden without permission from the copyrighted holder.

Library of Congress Control Number: 2025944678

International Standard Book Number: 979-8-89674-052-0

Masthof Press

219 Mill Road | Morgantown, PA 19543-9516
www.Masthof.com

The River Between Us is set in rural Vietnam from the 1930s to the post-war era, exploring the enduring bond between two childhood friends whose lives are fractured by war, politics, and personal betrayal. Minh and Mai grow up inseparable in a quiet village. But as colonial rule collapses and the country descends into chaos, their paths diverge. Minh becomes a mother and caretaker amid hardship, while Mai disappears into the shifting loyalties of a divided nation.

To all the women who survived the atrocities of war:

Your strength, resilience, and courage in the face of unimaginable horrors are truly inspiring. You have endured suffering that no one should ever have to experience, and your ability to not only survive but to also rebuild your lives and communities is a testament to the indomitable spirit of women.

You are mothers, daughters, sisters, friends, and leaders. You have faced violence, loss, displacement, and the destruction of everything you hold dear, yet you have persevered. You have cared for your families, advocated for your communities, and worked to rebuild shattered societies. Your stories deserve to be heard, and your contributions to peace and healing must be acknowledged and celebrated.

You are the embodiment of hope and the driving force for a better future. You are not alone. There are people and organizations dedicated to supporting you in your journey towards healing and recovery. Your strength and resilience remind us of the importance of peace, justice, and the protection of human rights for all.

This story is a work of fiction, but it is rooted in the heart of real places, real pain, and the real strength of Vietnamese families, especially women; who endured unspeakable losses and held on to joy wherever they could find it. *The River Between Us* was written to honor the quiet resilience of villages, mothers, daughters, and friendships that survived beyond war, hunger, and grief.

Minh and Mai are not just characters to me—they are voices of memory, sisterhood, and healing. Through bikes and lullabies, firelight and silence, this is their love story—not romantic, but life-saving.

This novel contains scenes involving wartime violence, famine, public executions, sexual assault, and adult relations. These are presented with care and emotional authenticity, never for shock value. Reader discretion is advised.

CONTENTS

Dedication—v

Author's Note—vi

Content Advisory—vi

Chapter 1: Dawn Over the Paddies.................................1

Chapter 2: The Ones Who Came Before 9

Chapter 3: Lanterns on the River 17

Chapter 4: The Butcher's Hands..................................25

Chapter 5: The Long Road to the Market.....................31

Chapter 6: What Cannot Be Mended............................ 41

Chapter 7: The Year of Empty Bowls 51

Chapter 8: Rice Girls of the Market 61

Chapter 9: The Age of Working 67

Chapter 10: The New Oppressor 81

Chapter 11: Beneath the Blossoms, Secrets Bloom....................87

Chapter 12: Price of Resistance 95

Chapter 13: My Brother's Battle 107

Chapter 14: Letters from the City................................113

Chapter 15: Independence Was in Our Grasp 123

Chapter 16: The Celebration of Ho Chi Minh 129

Chapter 17: The Day of Two Brides...............................133

Chapter 18: When the Fields Turned to Ash 137

Chapter 19: The Train to Forgiveness 141

Chapter 20: Arriving Home 151

Chapter 21: The Weight of Quiet Years 155

Chapter 22: The Second Independence 163

Chapter 23: The Weight of Independence 169

Chapter 24: The Red Dawn 175

Chapter 25: The Gathering Storm 183

Chapter 26: Word from the North and South 187

Chapter 27: Fractured Earth 193

Chapter 28: Mai's Husband 199

Chapter 29: The Invitation She Couldn't Bear 207

Chapter 30: The Secret Resistance 211

Chapter 31: Not My Daughter 219

Chapter 32: When the Rain Wouldn't Stop 223

Chapter 33: The Night the River Took Him 245

Chapter 34: The Children of Ash and Rain 251

Chapter 35: Riverboats and Puppet Strings 255

Chapter 36: The Harvest After War 259

Chapter 37: The Ones Who Remain 263

Epilogue—267

Author's Bio—271

CHAPTER 1

DAWN OVER THE PADDIES

1930 — Lang Duong Village,
near Hue city, Northern Vietnam

The first sounds I heard each morning were the crickets and grasshoppers, chirping beneath the veil of night, long before the sun rose over the rice paddies. It was a familiar rhythm—the pulse of our life in Lang Duong. That soft hum of nature slowly began to fade in the distance as the sun's hand stretched out across the vast forest and fertile lands around our home.

My father, Giang, was always the first to rise. Not just in our home, but in the entire village. Every morning, I would hear his dry cough as he cleared his throat. His footsteps were steady and purposeful, like the first heartbeat of the day. People often said he could hear the rice grow, that he was born with the spirit of the land in his bones. To me, he was a man of great strength and fortitude—a man who never complained, even when the rains came too soon or the harvests fell too thin.

As the sky began to brighten, painting the clouds with streaks of pink and orange, and the dew which collected throughout the night on our porch, you could hear the last cries of the cicadas slipping into silence. That moment, just before the birds began their morning chorus, was my favorite. It was like the world paused, listening, waiting.

The scent of wet soil drifted through the thin walls of our bamboo hut. It was the smell of life, of growth, of work and reward. Soon the cool air that the night provided would turn hot and humid as the sunshine crept into the slits of our siding, brightening our home, but in so doing, making it unbearably uncomfortable to be sitting inside throughout the day.

I stirred beneath the woven mat, blinking in the gloomy gray light of morning. My older brother, Khang, lay beside me, clutching the edge of his mat with one hand, his mouth slightly open. He breathed heavily, lost in dreams of playing village games with his friends. I sat up slowly and rubbed my eyes, glancing around our small dim room. The quiet creaking of the floorboards outside told me Mama was already awake.

Quickly, I laid back down and squeezed my eyes shut, pretending to sleep. The door hinges to our room creaked softly, letting me know someone had entered. A moment later, I felt the warmth of a soft hand on my hair and gliding across my face.

"Up, my little lotus," Mama whispered.

Her voice was soft as silk, but firm—like the tug of wind that bends the tallest stalks of rice. I yawned and sat up; her call impossible to ignore.

My mother, Linh, was a woman who embodied good nature and resilience. She wore her hair in a tight bun and her hands bore light scars of years working the fields, yet her touch was always gentle when it reached my cheek. She combed her fingers through my tangled hair and smiled.

"We have a busy day ahead. Gather your tools."

Outside, our world was cloaked in a delicate blue and silver—dawn draped over the hills like sheer cloth. The rice paddies shimmered like glass, reflecting the newborn light. Mist clung low to the ground, wrapping around the bamboo stilts of neighboring homes and drifting between water buffalo tracks in the mud.

Father was already outside, bent over the ox cart. He murmured something low and soft to the animal as he checked its harness, his rough palm brushing the beast's side like an old friend. His silhouette moved with slow grace—each step deliberate, each motion practiced from years of labor.

I fetched my thumb knife, worn smooth by my small fingers. I was still too young to wield the curved sickle like Father and Khang, but I didn't mind. The knife was mine, and it meant I had work to do. Important work.

Khang was awake now too, standing at the doorway in his patched cotton shirt. He yawned dramatically and lifted his machete above his head like a warrior. He pointed it at me.

"Gotcha!" he shouted, breaking into laughter.

His games were always loud, always foolish—but his heart was good. Without waiting, he leapt down the porch steps and took off down the path, his machete swinging by his side like a knight's sword.

I pulled on my mother's coarse tunic and followed her toward the field. We passed Bà ngoại's room—our grandmother—still dark and quiet. She would wake much later. As Father liked to say, "She's earned her rest."

Crossing the heart of our village, the ground beneath our feet changed from packed earth to wet clay as we climbed the narrow trail into the mist-veiled hills. The mountain paths were familiar to my parents, etched into their memory like calligraphy on rice paper. I stumbled once or twice on a hidden root, but Mama held my hand and led me gently. Following in foot was a puppy who often followed my brother Khang, who we named Hooch. We called him our own but in reality, he belonged to all the villagers. A stray who loved to wander home-to-home eating scraps. He took a particular liking to Khang and would follow us out to the fields each morning.

The fog thickened as we reached the higher terraces. It swallowed our feet and blanketed the rows of rice so only their tops poked through like little green flags in a sea of white.

At the paddies, frogs sprang from our steps, tiny brown flashes of life vanishing into the muck. The water was cold between my toes, and the air hummed with the buzz of insects waking up. Far beyond, the river sang softly, winding like a silk ribbon through the valley.

"Come, Minh," Father called, waving with one hand.

I ran to him, splashing through the mud, my feet kicking up water like rain. He smiled when I reached him and handed me a small bundle of seedlings.

"Today, we plant. The ancestors are smiling on us—be gentle."

I nodded solemnly. Planting was a sacred task, and even I knew that. The land gave life, but only if you treated it with respect.

We worked until the sun stood high above us, sweat pouring down our backs. The air thickened with heat, and the green rice leaves shimmered in waves. Father loaded sacks of grain onto the cart, grunting with each sack he carried but never complaining. In the mean-time Khang would give Hooch a belly rub and pat him on the head. Hooch liked to watch over us working the fields while he laid his head in the soil and wagged his tail.

When father finished loading the cart Khang would tell Hooch to go home and he would head back to the village, disappearing for the day. Then my family would walk together, taking the winding path down the mountain, the cart creaking behind us. Our bare feet slapped the dust-covered stones. I felt proud—part of something ancient and real. Our destination was the city of Hue to sell the fruits of our labor.

Huế was a city of timeless beauty, where history lingered in every stone. It stood as the imperial capital, our emperor Bao Dai from the Nguyen dynasty even allowed people to use his surname. The city was a place of literature, poetry, music, and art. The government took care of its citizens building bridges, roads, and canals to connect people and increase trade. They even implemented a national academy to teach Confucianism and Vietnamese history.

At its heart stood the Imperial Citadel, a vast walled complex surrounded by moats with majestic gates opening into a world of temples, gardens, and palaces. The innermost sanctuary, the Forbidden Purple City, held the imperial tombs of previous emperors. Its curved tile roofs, lacquered red pillars, and dragon motifs presented a past, steeped in tradition and ceremony. Lotus ponds shimmered beneath the sun, bonsai trees stood like sentinels in the courtyards, and the soft scent of sandalwood incense drifted throughout the grounds.

South of the river, the French Quarter carried its own elegance, ochre-walled villas and the Hue Railway Station. Across the Perfume River, the graceful Trường Tiền Bridge linking the old imperial city with the modern bustle beyond. The bridges iron arches and iron-wood base held the weight of daily life—cyclists, market vendors, schoolchildren, and lovers walking hand in hand.

At night, lanterns reflected on the water below, turning the river into a mirror of fireflies.

The market in Hue was loud and colorful. Vendors cried out prices, bartering in sing-song tones. The air was a swirl of fish, spices, roasted duck, and boiled sugarcane. Mama held our earnings tightly as she moved from stall to stall—picking out leafy greens, a chicken, a basket of eggs. On lucky days, pork belly too.

Father, as always, crossed the street to see Mr. Lao. They laughed like old friends, and Father bought a small sack of lychees for Bà ngoại. He always said the fruit reminded her of her girlhood, when she still climbed trees and danced barefoot through the river shallows.

As we left the city behind, and the road curved around the final bend toward Lang Duong, a familiar voice rang out like a bell.

"Minh!"

There, standing near the edge of the bamboo grove, was Mai—bright-eyed and barefoot as ever. Her hair was wild, her cheeks streaked with dust, and she waved a reed in her hand.

I dropped everything and ran to her.

We embraced in laughter as she became dirty from my mud-covered arms. The joy of seeing her filled my heart with something warm and endless. For a moment, nothing else mattered.

"I can help carry something!" Mai said, puffing out her chest like a proud ox, though she was barely heavier than a sack of rice.

Father chuckled. "My two little dragons," he said, his eyes crinkling. "Let's see how strong you really are."

He handed us a small bag of grain each, and we walked the rest of the way home together, stumbling and giggling under the weight.

Mai was more than a friend. She was my second shadow, my secret keeper, my other heartbeat. Our lives braided together from birth. Her father was a butcher. Her mother cooked for the village outside their home. They were kind people, hardworking and quiet. Education was a luxury in our village, but Father grew up in the city, and he knew many things. Each night he taught me—calligraphy, simple sums, counting numbers, and stories or folktales from old scrolls he use to read. I shared everything I learned with Mai.

On our days off, Mai and I roamed the hills. We played dragon and snake, cat and mouse, running until our feet were sore. But our best adventures happened far from watchful eyes—beyond the village, where the world had yet to be touched by man.

We chased butterflies and built stick houses hidden among the reeds. We whispered dreams into the wind, made bracelets of vines, and buried little treasures in secret spots we swore to remember forever.

"I'll never leave you," Mai once said, her hand in mine.

"Never," I promised.

We made a vow—etched in mud and memory—that nothing would ever break us apart.

But even in paradise, storms sometimes gather beyond the horizon.

And though we didn't know it yet, the first rumblings of change had already begun.

CHAPTER 2

THE ONES WHO CAME BEFORE

1932 — Lang Duong Village, near Hue

I was too young to remember my mother's parents.

I had never seen their faces—not in a photo, not in a drawing, not even in a rough carving. But they lived vividly in the stories Mama told, so often and so earnestly that I sometimes felt I could almost remember them too. In my mind's eye, they had rough, sun-darkened skin, calloused hands, and quiet strength. They were shaped by the same land we worked—strong, weathered, rooted.

"They gave us these fields," Mama would sometimes say as she stood barefoot at the edge of a paddy, her eyes scanning the muddy expanse. "Not just the mud and the seed, but the right to work for what's ours."

She'd say it almost like a prayer, like she wasn't speaking to me but to their lingering spirits.

They were taken by a fever that swept through the valley one spring, years before I was born. I often imagined that season—wet, gray, relentless—and how it must have felt to bury the ones you loved while the rain soaked the earth like a broken dam. But their legacy—the tools, the land, and the grit to keep going—took root deep in us.

Every morning, before the birds sang or the sun had fully broken through the haze, Mama would set a bowl of warm rice at the little altar in the corner of our home.

"For their spirits," she said, pressing her palms together in silence.

The smoke from a single stick of incense curled toward the rafters, mixing with the scent of the earth and wet rice still clinging to our clothes from the day before.

Sometimes in the fields, as we bent low under the sun, Mama would pause, rest her back, and raise her gaze toward the horizon.

"That tree," she'd say, pointing to a knobby old tamarind swaying lazily near the paddies, "my mother planted it when I was your age."

She'd smile then, but there was always something behind it. A memory she didn't speak aloud.

I never dared touching it without permission.

It was my grandfather who, long ago, had cleared the swampy land with little more than a shovel, a bamboo bucket, and a patient buffalo. He had dammed the creek with rocks he carried by hand and dug out channels that now watered our fields each season. My grandmother, even while pregnant, had planted the first crop of rice with her bare hands, her swollen feet pressed into the cool mud, and still found the breath to sing lullabies as she worked.

They left behind no gold, no silk, no inheritance but this—the land.

And the will to work it.

Sometimes I asked Mama what her mother was like.

"She was sharper than me," she'd say, then soften. "But she

sang more, too. Sang to me when I had night fevers. Songs her mother sang. French melodies, but our words."

I asked her to sing them.

She did.

Ru Con Trong Gió
(Lullaby in the Wind)

Gió ru con ngủ trên vành trăng xưa,
Mẹ ngồi nhớ cha phương trời xa mù.
Đêm sâu rơi lệ theo khói lam chiều,
Mơ ngày đoàn tụ, mơ cánh diều bay.

The wind rocks you to sleep beneath an old moon,
Mother sits remembering a father lost far away.
Deep into the night, her tears drift like evening cooking smoke.
She dreams of reunion, dreams of kites flying again.

The song continued:

Ngủ đi con, gió ru buồn buồn,
Cỏ khô lặng lẽ bên bờ ruộng vắng.
Chim không hót nữa, trăng thôi không tròn,
Mẹ ru lời vắng, cho con giấc lành.

Sleep now, my child, the wind sings its sorrow.
Dry grass stands quietly beside the empty rice field.
The birds no longer sing, and the moon is no longer full.
Mother hums soft, lonely words to give you peaceful dreams.

They were haunting and lovely, almost lullabies, even when they carried sorrow.

Mama also spoke of her older brother, Po, with a kind of fond mischief that softened her voice.

He was tall, she said, always dirty, always smiling, and always up to no good—but never cruel.

"When we were children," Mama laughed once, "he would sit on the riverbank and let leeches crawl up his legs just to fish them off and use them as bait. He'd wave them in my face, pretend to eat them, and I would scream every time."

She giggled at the memory, wiping sweat from her brow, and for a moment she was just a girl again, running barefoot along the stream.

Now Uncle Po lived on the far edge of the village. He no longer worked the paddies but ran a rubber plantation—rows and rows of thin, white-barked trees whose sap bled slowly into tiny bowls. When we visited, he showed us how the latex oozed from the grooves he carved into the bark.

"See, little ones," he said once, kneeling beside a tree, "you don't just chop it down and poof—it's rubber. It takes patience. You pull it out little by little, and even then, it's soft, useless. Until you mix it with acid and give it time to harden."

His wife, Aunt Tam, usually said little, but her hands were quick and sure, always stirring something in a basin, always working beside him.

Their newborn daughter, Nguyet—which meant "moon"—was still wrapped in blankets most days, her cries as tiny as her fingers, which I loved to hold.

My brothers and I called her "Nugget" when no one was listening. To us she was a precious nugget of gold, which we always wanted to hold.

On my father's side, things had been different.

They owned a rickshaw business in the city—not wealth, exactly, but a steady living. It was through this business that Mama and Papa first met. The story of their meeting was one Father loved to tell, and each time, the details shifted just a little.

"She was the prettiest girl in the market," he'd say, "selling rice like she was royalty."

He was pulling a merchant to the docks and stopped near her stall to drink water. She was wiping her neck with a red handkerchief, the sweat glistening on her temple.

My father was instantly captivated by my mother's beauty. He could even remember what she was wearing that day. A brown work shirt, straw hat, red handkerchief, and oversized khaki trousers.

"I told her right then," Papa would say, grinning as he reenacted the scene, "'I'm going to marry you someday.'"

"And I told him he was full of frogs," Mama would chime in, laughing.

Mother said it didn't take long for her feelings to mature for Father either.

In the market, mom would watch dad run customers up and down the street all day. When they crossed paths, he would always give her a smile and tip his hat.

Mom told me every time he tipped that damn hat her heart melted a little inside.

Overtime, Father would visit Mother at her village during his downtime. He would end up getting stuck as a labor hand threshing the grain.

Mother's father didn't think dad would be able to work hard with his hands since he was a city boy, but my dad proved himself worthy. I guess pulling a rickshaw all those years made my father build a strong enough body, to labor in the fields.

Their first date was a water puppet show by the lotus lake—wooden figures dancing over water, music floating from the shadows.

Mama said she was nervous. Papa said he couldn't stop watching her, not the puppets.

Eventually, Father gave up his rickshaw and his city life. He moved to Mama's village to be part of the world she cherished. They married under a fabric arch in front of the ancestral altar.

He became a farmer, and though the calluses on his hands were different than the ones from pulling rickshaws, they were no less real.

His father, my other grandfather, passed away not long after—a stroke, they said.

Grandfather was a cunning business man, and it was said he was educated. I guess that is how my father learned to read and write. He ran a rickshaw business in the city.

He owned a small fleet of rickshaws and a storefront where workers would gather each morning. My grandmother helped manage the coins, kept track of the day's earnings, and boiled soup for the drivers at midday.

My only surviving grandparent is my father's mother.

My grandmother, left alone and weary, sold the business and moved to the countryside with only a few belongings: a jade bangle, a portrait, some linens, and the last rickshaw—not to ride, but to remember.

She kept her dignity tucked inside her silence and her stories, and with her came the smell of lotus tea and old lavender.

At night, I would curl up in her lap. Her songs were like the wind brushing over dry reeds.

"Ru con, ru con..."

Sleep, child. Sleep.

She always had a ginger candy in her sleeve, which she would slip into my hand even while Mama scolded, "You'll rot her teeth, Bà ngoại."

That spring, the rains came early. They soaked the earth red and fattened the rivers. Life, already hard, became heavier.

Mother would sit Khang and I down with Father and Grandmother one night, smiling and looking into my father's eyes mother turned to us and said, "I'm pregnant, you will both be having another little brother or sister soon." Excitement could be felt in my nerves and bones. I began imagining the possibility of having a little brother or sister I could dress up, feed, or carry around the house.

But I'd have to wait, Mother was only beginning to show, meaning she had months before delivering the baby.

Still, the fields needed tending. There were no days off. Not even for Mama, though her belly had begun to swell, the skin stretched tight over the child growing inside.

In the mornings grandmother and I would get up to prepare food, as we tried to allow mother to rest. I would pack the fruits and tie the rice in banana leaves. These were snacks I'd carry in my pack for our lunch breaks in the hot sun while working in the fields. I'd help scrub the radishes, while grandmother peeled the rest, often at supper we would have rice, a salad, and soup. I took pride in knowing that I helped prepare things in the kitchen for my family.

As time rolled on, I could see Mother looked fatigued behind her constant smile. Mother use to carry water back from the village well to help Grandmother and I clean the vegetables but since I knew how to boil the rice and the greens, I would fetch the water for mother.

One evening mother would clutch her belly and fall to her knees after eating dinner. Her breathing became heavy and she looked to my father in despair, "Get the midwife, quickly" she urged. Father sprang to his feet, running barefoot into the storm. By the time he returned, soaked to the bone, the sky had cracked with lightning.

The midwife—a short, stern woman from down the road—rushed to Mama's side.

Mother was laying on her bedding, which was soaked in blood. The wet nurse turned to me and my brother and said, "Get some clean clothes, quickly children." I searched as quickly as I could, Grandmother handed me a fresh cloth and we cleared the space around Mother's bed. Then Grandmother took my hand. "This is no place for a child, come with me."

Grandmother held me and Khang tight, ushering us to the corner of the room.

"You shouldn't have to see this," she murmured, rocking me as she tried to blanket our eyes with her fingers while Mama screamed out in pain behind the woven curtain.

The sounds were terrible. My heart pounded with every groan, every command: "Push! Push! It's almost here!"

And then—a cry.

Sharp and strong. The sound of new life.

I held my breath and looked up at Grandmother. Her eyes were damp.

"He's here," she whispered. "Your baby brother."

In that moment, the storm outside faded to a hush.

Inside our little bamboo hut, something ancient and beautiful had begun again.

CHAPTER 3

LANTERNS ON THE RIVER

*Mid-Autumn Festival, 1932—
Lang Duong Village*

The air smelled of roasting sweet potatoes and river mud—a scent that clung to your skin and nestled in your memory. It was the kind of smell that meant something special was coming.

Mai's father who I considered my uncle, was helping raise a massive dragon puppet for the parade. My brother Khang strung lanterns through tree branches with rope made from bamboo fibers. My grandmother stood on our porch with a basin of tea, humming as she watched the festival unfold.

I ran barefoot down the dusty path my small hands wrapped tightly around a bundle of bamboo sticks and delicate paper lanterns. The ends poked at my sides, but I didn't care. Behind me, Mai stumbled over a rock and let out a squeal, then sprinted to catch up, laughing breathlessly. Our arms were full of fragile lanterns shaped like birds, fish, and lotus blossoms. One being crushed under the weight of my arm.

"It's September!" she gasped between giggles. "You'll crush them, Minh!"

But I only laughed harder, kicking up dust behind me. My heart beat like a drum in my chest. Tonight was the Mid-Autumn Festival—*Tết Trung Thu*—the most magical night of the year. Even the grown-ups, who always seemed tired and stern, seemed softer on nights like this.

The village square glowed with excitement. Vendors had set up makeshift stalls under canopies of silk and straw. The air buzzed with the calls of sellers shouting: "Sugarcane juice! Fresh lychees! Bamboo toys for clever hands!"

Women in bright silk tunics sold mooncakes filled with mung bean paste and salted egg yolks, their trays piled high like treasure. Children reached eagerly as their parents bartered with coins or rice grains. The scent of charred scallion pancakes, grilled pork skewers, and cinnamon-scented sticky rice mingled in the air.

Drummers paraded past, their rhythms pounding into our chests like thunder. One of the older boys twirled a fire stick, drawing wide arcs that illuminated faces in amber flashes. The dragon puppet—longer than three water buffalo—wound its way through the crowd, its eyes glowing red, its scales were glimmering beads of yellow and orange. We cheered as it dipped and danced.

As the sun was slipping behind the hills, painting the sky in streaks of gold and lavender. In the heart of the village, families gathered on woven mats. Mothers unwrapped banana leaves filled with taro root, sticky rice cakes, jackfruit seeds, and mangosteens. Elders passed around tiny porcelain cups of green tea. Everywhere, the lanterns flickered: turtles, phoenixes, stars, each one a wish waiting to be released. Children chased each other between the homes, laughing with faces slick with syrup and sweat, glowing like fireflies in the fading light.

Lanterns bobbed above the rooftops—red, yellow, pink, and

gold—hanging from bamboo poles and doorframes. They swayed gently in the breeze, casting soft halos over the thatched huts. The old banyan tree stood proudly in the square, its thick roots twisting into the earth like ancient fingers. From one of its wide branches hung the village drum, silent for now.

Mai and I found my family's mat beneath that tree. Mama sat cross-legged, cradling baby Bo in her arms, humming softly. Her hair was pulled back in a loose knot, and sweat clung to her neck and temples. My brother Khang sat beside her, cheeks full of sticky rice, already halfway through his second cake. He didn't even stop chewing when we plopped down beside him.

Father crouched at the edge of the mat, sipping tea, his face relaxed in a way I didn't often see. His calloused hands rested on his knees, and the faintest smile tugged at the corners of his lips.

"Did you finish the lanterns?" he asked, his eyes crinkling as he looked at me.

I nodded proudly and unfolded the crumpled bundle in my arms. "Mai helped me," I said, giving her a gentle nudge. She grinned and plopped down beside me, brushing a smear of dirt from her cheek.

Father picked up one of the lanterns—a delicate swan with wings of folded rice paper and bamboo ribs so thin you could see the lantern's shadow dance behind it.

"Beautiful," he said, turning it slowly in his hands. "Just like you."

I felt my cheeks warm. Mai and I giggled and whispered to each other as we nibbled the sweet treats we had hidden in our sleeves—dried plums and peanut candies we'd swiped from the edge of the mat.

Then I looked up and asked quietly, "Will Uncle Po be coming?"

Mama's smile faltered. She shifted Bo gently on her lap and met my eyes. "Not tonight, dear."

No explanation. Just that.

I was disappointed, hoping that I would see my cousin Nguyet.

As the moon climbed above the tree line, round and yellow as an egg yolk, the procession began.

Men dressed in elaborate costumes marching with torches and lanterns in hand, others playing string and musical instruments. They danced and performed while tossing small candies to us in the crowd. Then came Uncle Hung, leading the dragon's head, as Mai pointed and smiled, shouting, "Dad!" Waving to make sure he saw us. The dragon paused, swaying in front of us a few extra moments—Uncle Hung making sure Mai and I had the best view, before he continued leading the procession.

When the demonstration ended, the village headman stepped forward. His robes rustled as he raised his hands, and he struck the drum three times.

BONG.

BONG.

BONG.

The sound rang through the air like thunder rolling over hills.

Children squealed and grabbed their lanterns. I clutched my swan and leapt to my feet. Mai and I ran hand-in-hand to the riverbank, careful not to drop or tear our creations. The path was lined with torches, their flames bending toward the water as if drawn by the current.

At the water's edge, I knelt in the mud. The river glimmered in the moonlight, slow and glassy, its surface beginning to sparkle with floating lights. All around us, children were lighting lanterns, one by one, their faces solemn as they whispered their wishes.

Father came up behind me, crouched low, and lit a stick of incense. The glowing tip burned a soft gold in the dark. He held it out toward me.

"Take your time," he murmured. "Lanterns are delicate. Like hopes."

I held my breath and leaned in. My hands trembled as I touched the flame to the candle inside the swan. For a moment, nothing happened. Then—a flicker. A bloom of warm light in the hollow of the paper belly.

The swan lantern came to life, its wings glowing faintly, its paper tail curling like a feather.

"Make your wish, my daughter," Father said softly, placing his hand on my back.

I closed my eyes. The night was so quiet I could hear the river lapping the shore.

Please let Mama and Papa live forever.

Please let Khang and Bo grow up strong.

Please let Mai and I stay together, always.

When I opened my eyes, the swan lantern shimmered. I set it gently on the water. It bobbed once, uncertain—then the current took it. Slowly, it glided downstream, joining the hundred other lights drifting across the dark. The river looked like a sky turned upside down.

I stood, watching until the swan vanished into the mist.

Later, music floated over the village—bamboo flutes and zithers, the rhythm of drums and laughter. Children danced in circles, swinging paper dragons. The air smelled of smoke and sweet rice.

But I noticed something else—a group of men gathered under

the banyan tree, half-shadowed in torchlight. Their voices were low. Their faces serious.

Among them: Father.

And Uncle Po.

My heart leapt. I hadn't seen him all night, and there he was—his tall frame hunched slightly forward, his jaw tight, his eyes not smiling. Something about the way they stood made my chest feel tight.

I tugged on Mai's sleeve. "Mai, Mai! It's Uncle Po. I'm going to say hello."

Before I could take a step, Mai's father—Uncle Hung—reached out and caught my arm.

"Just hold up there," he said gently. "Where do you think you're going?"

"To see my uncle," I said. "I just want to say hi."

He shook his head slowly. "Best wait here, little sparrow. They're having a grown-up chat over there."

I frowned and turned to Mai. "What are they talking about?"

Mai shrugged. "My papa says the French made new taxes. Even for the rice we grow."

I didn't understand.

The French had always been here. Tall men in tight fatigues, their boots caked with dust. Sometimes they rode horses through the market, shouting words no one understood. Sometimes they smiled and bought lychees. Other times they pushed people aside without a glance.

Mother had told me early on: Don't look them in the eye.

Now, the whispers were growing louder. They floated through the village like smoke from a distant fire.

Whispers of unfairness.

Of men disappearing.

Of rebellion.

The drum sounded again—three quick strikes, calling the children back. We ran to the others and joined the circle dance, arms linked, lanterns bobbing in time with the song. We laughed and shouted, our joy rising up like sparks into the sky.

But as I spun, I caught a glimpse of Father's face in the firelight—quiet, strained, as if something heavy pressed behind his eyes.

That was the first time I felt it—not fear, not exactly, but something close. A tremor under the surface of the joy.

Something was coming.

Something bigger than me, bigger than the lanterns, the river, even the full moon overhead.

But for that moment, Mai's fingers were warm in mine. The air was full of music. The night was full of wishes.

And so, I let it go.

Just for tonight.

CHAPTER 4

THE BUTCHER'S HANDS

Lang Duong Village, late 1932

If Mai was like my sister, then her family was like my second home.

As much time as Mai spent in my house—chasing Khang through the yard, cradling baby Bo while Mama hung laundry—I spent just as many afternoons in hers. Their home always smelled of lemongrass, charcoal, and something sweet bubbling in a pot. It was smaller than ours but always full—of laughter, voices, smoke, food, and life.

There was no man in the village more solid than Mai's father, Uncle Hung. His shoulders were broad like an ox, and when he laughed, it was a rumble that seemed to come from the soles of his feet. His arms were as thick as tree trunks, with veins like the roots of the banyan tree, and yet he moved with a quiet grace, especially when he held a knife.

Hung wasn't just a butcher. He was a keeper of life—and of death.

He raised every animal he slaughtered, with hands that fed, cleaned, and cradled them long before they reached the chopping block. When the time came, he whispered to them—words I didn't understand—and when the blade fell, he bowed his head in thanks.

"Every life should be respected," he told me once, after carving a duck with precise, tender strokes. We sat on low stools beneath the awning of his home. The skin crackled, the meat still steaming.

"Never let a good meal go to waste," he added, dropping an extra piece into my bowl with a wink.

I always ate well at Mai's.

Their small farm sat on the edge of the village, a tangle of mud paths and bamboo fencing. Ducks waddled freely beneath the stilts of their house. Chickens pecked near the well. There was always at least one goat bleating about something. When I arrived, Mai would wave me over from the kitchen hut, her hands covered in rice flour or fish paste, her cheeks glowing from the fire.

"Minh!" she'd call. "Come help! Mama's making something special!"

Mai's mother, Lianne, had a quiet, steady presence—not loud, but always felt. Her food was famous in the village, especially her braised pork belly, caramelized until the edges stuck to your teeth and melted on your tongue. She slow-cooked everything in clay pots over open flame, stirring with one hand while balancing a basket of herbs with the other.

She always welcomed me like a daughter.

"Minh, wash the mint leaves, would you? And tell your mother to send me more ginger if she's got any."

"Yes, Auntie Lianne," I'd say, smiling as I rolled up my sleeves.

Her cooking hut was more than a kitchen—it was a gathering place. Bamboo benches lined the edge where neighbors would perch, gossiping over bowls of noodle soup or grilled catfish wrapped in banana leaves. The butcher and the cook—that's how people thought of Mai's parents. But to me, they were home. The way they teased each other, the way Lianne clicked her tongue when Hung got too generous with meat portions. The way Hung called me his half-daughter whenever I asked for seconds.

"You eat like your half mine anyway!" he'd laugh, slapping his knee. I'd blush, pretending to be embarrassed while stealing a glance at Mai, who always grinned and rolled her eyes at him.

Sometimes I would arrive early in the morning, just as the sky began to warm. Lianne would already be pounding garlic in a stone mortar, while Mai ground lemongrass with rhythmic grace, humming a tune passed down from her grandmother. I would join them wordlessly, falling into the familiar rhythm. It felt like something sacred.

During the day, their front porch became a kind of marketplace. Villagers came not just to buy food, but to talk. Women leaned close, fanning themselves as they whispered about engagements, feuds, and dreams. Men lingered longer than necessary over bowls of soup, talking about weather, harvests, and the latest village mischief.

"Did you hear?" Mai would whisper to me between serving bowls. "Old Thien's son is marrying the flower girl from up the river."

Or: "Mrs. Duong says her brother was drunk again. Tried to ride a pig through the fields!"

We'd stifle giggles as we cleared bowls or fanned the fire.

But over time, the gossip began to change. The stories turned quieter, darker.

No longer just about weddings or drunken antics—now, there were rumors about disappearances, secret meetings, men slipping away at night. There was talk of revolutionaries. Freedom fighters. Guerillas who moved like shadows through the jungle, striking at French outposts and vanishing before dawn.

Lianne kept her voice low when these conversations happened, but I saw her eyes—alert, worried. Hung, usually so warm, grew quieter at dinner. Once, I heard him say softly to her, "If we lose the boys to the hills, what will be left for the girls?"

Mai's cousin, Sahn, only seventeen, disappeared one night. His mother came sobbing to Lianne's kitchen, hands trembling as she clutched a worn sandal.

"He took nothing," she cried. "Not even his blanket."

The French were everywhere these days—boots in the market, rifles near the schoolhouse. They barked in strange accents and taxed our rice, our fish, even our salt. Mama said they taxed our dignity. Papa said nothing, but his eyes grew darker with each passing day.

One afternoon, I sat beneath the kitchen eaves, peeling shallots with Mai. Lianne stirred a pot nearby, humming a lullaby.

"Do you think the French will go away?" I asked, my voice barely above a whisper.

Mai stopped peeling.

"I don't know," she said. "But my papa says they won't leave unless we make them."

I thought of the night of the lantern festival—of my father's face in the firelight, shadowed and strained. Of Uncle Po standing among the men near the banyan tree.

Fear settled in my belly again like cold rice. I didn't know what war looked like. I didn't know how a village like ours could stand up to something as big as France.

But I knew this—something was changing.

And it was coming for all of us—even in the safety of kitchens, even in the warmth of borrowed families.

CHAPTER 5

THE LONG ROAD TO THE MARKET

The morning the soldiers came, the river had overflowed in the night with rain. Whispers of unrest had reached our secluded village. The French colonial authorities had intensified their crackdowns on suspected revolutionaries, and the atmosphere was thick with fear.

I awoke to the sound of Mama's voice, sharp and anxious, calling for Khang to fetch more rope to tie down the cart. The storm had blown through, leaving the paddies flooded, the paths muddy and treacherous. But the rice still needed to be sold.

Father stood by the ox cart, adjusting the heavy sacks of grain. His shirt clung to him, soaked through from hauling the sacks from the storage shed to prevent them from molding. He was going to the market alone today—Mama was still nursing Bo, and he worried that Khang or I might catch a cold.

Mama pressed a bundle of sticky rice into Dad's hands. "Eat on the road," she said gently. Dad kissed her forehead, waved goodbye to each of us, and set off up the mountain. The ox lumbered forward, leaving deep hoof marks in the mud as the cart creaked behind it.

The journey to the market usually took two hours. Today, with the road half-washed away, it would take longer.

Halfway there, Father pulled the ox to a stop. Ahead, a group of armed men blocked the path. Not French soldiers—but Vietnamese, rough and stern-faced. Their clothes bore no insignia, just torn hats and battered muskets. One stepped forward.

"We require your rice for the cause," he said.

Father's jaw clenched. "This rice feeds my family."

Another man stepped forward; palm open. "Rice," he repeated.

Father recognized one of the group: Chu, a boy from our village. His father sold fish at the market and my father often traded with him. Chu looked away, but not before giving Father a silent, pleading look.

Before Father could protest, the others moved in, untying the sacks of rice with swift hands. When they were done, they disappeared into the jungle, leaving the cart and my father empty handed.

Father stood still. His shoulders sagged. Days of work—gone. But he clicked his tongue at the ox and moved forward. He believed the French officials would investigate if he reported the theft.

At the market, French soldiers stood tall and cold-eyed in their blue coats. One noticed the empty cart and barked in French.

Father understood the words—but not the tone. Accusation. Threat.

The officer marched up, shouting and jabbing a finger into his chest. Father explained in French, "I'm here to report some thieves."

"Thieves, really?" the officer sneered. "You're going with that excuse?"

"It's not an excuse. It is the truth."

The soldier's tone grew darker. "Don't get smart with me." He grabbed Father's arm and twisted it behind his back, dragging him into the station.

Though Father spoke fluent French, taught to him by his own father, the soldiers only saw a Vietnamese peasant. Inside, he tried to explain to the interpreter what happened, but the French accused him of aiding rebels. His words were dismissed.

When he refused to sign a confession, he was told he would be detained until a trial—or until proven innocent. He tried to walk out. A soldier struck him in the face with the butt of a rifle, sending him sprawling.

Father was dragged away, thrown into a cell with other men— older farmers, traders—all accused of conspiring with the rebels simply because they had grain and produce missing from their stores or carts as well.

At home, Mama stood in the yard collecting fruits when a man returned with Father's ox and cart. He couldn't meet her eyes as he spoke.

"Your husband...he's been arrested."

Mama dropped the berries she had cradled in her shirt.

"I need some money to try and get him released," she said, her voice thin with desperation.

The man shook his head. "It won't do any good."

"Visiting hours are over, miss," he added gently. "You won't be able to see him until morning."

Shaking her head in worry, Mama turned silently and walked back into the house.

That night, the house felt unbearably empty. It was too late to visit the jail, so Mama and Grandmother planned to go in the morning. I lay awake on my mat, listening to the low murmur of their voices at the table—words filled with fear and a fragile hope that somehow, Father might be released.

I could hear Mama packing clothes and food throughout the night.

The next morning, French soldiers arrived in our village, dressed in crisp blue and white uniforms, their boots kicking up clouds of dust as they marched in.

"We are here to search for rebels," one of them announced.

They entered our home without asking, overturning baskets, pulling up floor mats, and poking through our sacks of rice.

Khang clung to me while Bo wrapped his arms around my legs, crying.

"When will Father come home?" Khang asked Mama.

She didn't answer—only shook her head slowly, her face tight with worry.

When the soldiers finished their search, they informed Mama that father was being held for aiding the rebel cause—an accusation that carried the possibility of a harsh sentence, even death.

Without hesitation, Mama went to the jar where she hid her savings. She handed the money to one of the soldiers. Her voice cracked as she pleaded, "Please...my husband is innocent. Please tell them. Please help him."

The French soldier took the money and tucked it into his left breast pocket.

"We will, ma'am. We will," he said with a genuine look before leaving the house.

The news of Father's arrest shattered Grandmother's heart anew. She hadn't cried when her husband died. She hadn't cried when she left her home in the city. But when she heard her son was in jail, she wept as if her bones were splintering apart.

Mama went to the jail the next day, desperate to see Father, but they refused her entry for several days. When she finally spoke to one of the French interpreters, she explained that she had paid the soldiers—that they had promised to speak on her husband's behalf.

"They lied," the interpreter said flatly. "No one has spoken for your husband. The investigation will continue until he's proven innocent...or someone else confesses."

Mama wailed then, broken by the betrayal. The soldiers had taken everything—her trust, her savings, her hope—and left her with nothing. But still, she would not give up. Not on him.

At home, Mother tried to soften our concerns, we constantly asked her where Papa had gone, if he was okay, and when he would be home. Mama always tried to distract us by playing a game or offering to make us food, instead of telling us what was really happening. Trying to shield us the only way she knew how. Sometimes weeks would pass where we heard nothing. Mother carried the burden alone, trying to protect us from the pain she felt.

Each day, she walked with Grandmother to the prison, bringing rice balls wrapped in banana leaves, sometimes nothing but salted water.

Grandma was small and hunched over, her eyes always red. At the prison gate, she pressed her hand to the bars and whispered, "Still my son. He is still mine." Her voice trembled, but the words held a fierce, unshakable truth.

Grandma's heartfelt words rang in my father' ears like threads of warmth in a place gone cold. They passed the rusted metal fence, past the stink of sweat and damp stone, and touched the other men, who wept for their own mothers and wives. They weren't just words. They were proof. Proof that someone still believed they were more than prisoners, more than accusations, more than forgotten.

The prison loomed over the market like a scar. Most people averted their eyes as they walked past, as if even glancing at it might draw suspicion. The walls were thick stone, stained with moss, and iron gates that cast long shadows.

Inside the prison walls my father's treatment was harsh. He was chained by the ankle to a stone bed only inches above the concrete floor. They were given no blankets or headrests. The men in the cell were spaced exactly two feet apart, row after row—forty to a cell, with barely enough room to lie flat. Rats scurried along the edges. Sometimes they gnawed through the straw mats or nipped at blistered feet. To relieve themselves, the men passed around a single metal bucket, emptied once each morning. The air was thick with the stench of rot, mold, and unwashed flesh. Even at night, the heat and humidity clung to the skin like a wet cloth. No breeze reached past the stone. The only relief from the heat came from the cold hard stone they slept on. If sleep, even came at all. Sleep was shallow and broken, the night air filled with groans, coughing, and the restless shifting of men.

Each morning, Father was dragged out to break stones under the sun. If he faltered, a guard lashed his back. He learned not to cry out—only to bite down and remember our faces.

While Father endured his punishment behind stone walls, we fought our own battles in the fields. Mama took up dad's work. She rose before dawn to tend the fields with Bo on her hip. Khang and I worked beside her, our hands small but determined. The rice wilted. Weeds took hold. Our fingers ached.

Whether it was sunny or rainy, we worked. At times, the mud

rose above our ankles and shins, sucking at our steps like it wanted to keep us there forever. In the heat, our feet split open with cuts from sharp reeds, the water stinging like vinegar. Blisters formed between our toes, soft at first, then angry and raw. The sun beat down on our necks until our skin peeled in patches. Working the fields without Dad made us work twice as hard for half as much.

Every evening, Mama brought what little food she could spare to the prison. Sticky rice, boiled greens, sometimes a piece of mango. She bribed guards to let him come to the gate. They sneered, searched her, then allowed it.

She pressed her forehead to the bars and whispered, "We are still here. We are waiting for you."

He would try to smile. Sometimes he couldn't lift his head.

Mother knew she needed to work hard. Her sole purpose was to farm and visit Father.

She stopped nursing Bo to shoulder the burden of the farm and market. I became Bo's mother in her place—bathing him, feeding him, singing him to sleep.

Mai would even come over to help bathe him, fed him porridge, and we took turns singing to him when he cried.

Mai's presence during the day lifted my spirits from the emptiness I felt missing my father.

I wanted to visit him, but Mama never let us. Only once did she get stern with me, "Stop asking," she said, "it's too dreadful a place for you to visit."

At night, I'd lay awake, listening to Mama's silent weeping.

Father had lost a noticeable amount of weight when Mother visited him. When Father grew thin, he asked for cigarettes. He never smoked before, but said they were valuable for trade. Mother would continue to bribe the guards to sneak him food and on occasion a pack of cigarettes.

Soon trading cigarettes turned to him smoking them. As Mom visited and could notice the smell on his prison uniform. For the first time in months, he felt like he could have control over something. Being locked up for so long, not controlling where and what you eat, where you sleep, and where to go to the bathroom was too much for a man who lived and worked in the fields.

Inside, the food was little more than thin soup and stale bread. My father's once-strong frame began to shrink, his shoulders hollowing, his eyes sunken from hunger.

One high-ranking guard seemed to hate him most of all. He once told my father that the men who had stolen his grain were fighting in the mountains—blowing up supply trucks, scrawling slogans of resistance across walls and bridges.

"Don't worry," the guard sneered. "Your friends will be joining you soon."

But my father was educated. And worse—he spoke his mind. Every time he answered back, it fueled the guard's cruelty.

One day, the guard made him count to ten in French.

With each number, he struck my father's leg with a club.

Un. Crack.

Deux. Crack.

Trois. Crack.

By the time he reached *dix*, his left leg had gone stiff from the repeated blows. It began to drag behind him, useless.

At home, Mama lied to us. She said there was a mix-up and that now Father was helping the French sort out local disputes, because of how educated he was. For a time, we all believed it. Even Grandmother who had stopped visiting the prison because of how it made her feel, started believing it. She smiled again, and spoke like Father's work was important. We all wanted to believe in the lie, because it was much easier than facing the truth.

During those long months while Father was away, something began to change in Khang. He became a little more rebellious, a little less like the quiet boy we knew. He started coming home later, ignoring Mama's requests, and spent his afternoons chasing Hooch through the village, determined to find out where the dog lived.

But Hooch always slipped away. So one day, when Khang finally caught him, he tied the dog to our porch with a rope. That night, Hooch howled endlessly, his mournful cries echoing through the dark, driving me and Grandmother mad. By morning, the rope was chewed clean through, and Hooch was gone again.

Khang wanted Hooch for himself. He didn't like sharing the dog with the rest of the village, where Hooch came and went as he pleased, loved by everyone and owned by no one. When Mama returned and saw what Khang had done, she didn't scold him in anger, she broke down crying. "Don't cage an animal," she said softly, "when it wants to run free."

Her words lingered and stuck with both of us. For a long time afterward, Khang and I would sit in silence, wondering if she had meant more than just the dog—if she was thinking of Father too, chained like an animal while the rest of the world kept moving.

Then, one ordinary day, Father came home. Just like that. No warning, no messenger, he simply appeared, standing in the doorway like a ghost returned from war. We later learned that Chu, the village boy who had helped steal the rice, had been cap- tured during a rebel raid. During his interrogation, he confessed to the theft and insisted Father be freed. He told them Father had no part in the rebellion, that he had been wrongly accused, wrongly imprisoned, wrongly tortured.

The interpreters persuaded the French captain to release my father.

But Chu—only fifteen years old—would take his place in prison.

The day Father returned home, I barely recognized him. He limped through the gate, thinner than a shadow, his clothes hanging loose on his frame. Yet in his eyes, his gaze remained unbroken.

I ran to him and wrapped my arms around his frail body, careful not to squeeze too tightly. He smelled of damp stone and ash, like a man who had lived underground.

Still, he was home.

But Chu was not.

Just a month after my father's release, Chu was executed by firing squad.

And though my father had been freed, I knew part of him never truly left that prison. He bore the guilt of Chu's sacrifice in silence, his heart heavy with the knowledge that someone else had to die, so he could live.

CHAPTER 6

WHAT CANNOT BE MENDED

The days after Father's return were strange. He was home but he wasn't really home. If something fell to the floor it was if he was shell shocked, his body would tense in fear of being hit. Not only was he mentally changed but he had physical changes as well.

His left leg dragged behind him like an oar. He no longer joined us in the fields. He sat often in the doorway, staring at the paddies or humming old songs under his breath, tunes from the city of Hue, during his youth.

He was thinner than a scarecrow, his skin stretched tight over his bones, his hair gray at the temples.

At first, I was overjoyed just to have him back—to sit beside him on the porch, to listen to his soft breathing at night.

But something inside him had broken. I watching him struggle to lift a water bucket, seeing him pause halfway up the porch steps to catch his breath, I began to understand that some things, once broken, never heal the same way.

My father was no longer the strong man who worked tirelessly on the fields. His injuries were so bad from his time spent in prison that he couldn't help much on the farm.

He no longer rose before the sun.

He no longer laughed at Khang's jokes or sang lullabies to baby Bo.

He no longer read books, or quizzed us on our calligraphy.

He spent most of his days staring at the horizon, smoking thin cigarettes rolled from corn husks, his eyes distant.

Grandmother wanted to desperately rouse his spirits and decided on throwing a feast, to commemorate his release. Even though we barely had food, she and Mama boiled every scrap of rice, dug for roots, and traded for a small piece of mackerel fish.

Although my father limped, and still barely spoke—he ate with both hands. He wept once, when Bà served him steamed taro, his favorite childhood food.

She smiled, pressing her hand to his cheek.

"My strong boy," she whispered. "You came home."

For a few hours that evening, glimpses of my old father flickered through. He told Bo a story about a clever rabbit. He hummed while Mama served the taro. When Khang made a joke about the neighbors' rooster, Father's mouth almost curved into a smile.

"See?" Grandmother whispered to me, clearing dishes. "He's still in there."

I nodded, but I noticed how quickly he tired. How his hands shook when he reached for his tea. How he kept glancing toward the door, as if something might come through it.

That night, I heard him talking to Mama in their room.

"I dream about them," he said. "The men who didn't come home. I see their faces."

"You're here now," Mama replied. "That's what matters."

"But why me? Why did I live when they didn't?"

I pressed my ear closer to the wall, but Mama's response was too soft to hear.

For weeks Grandmother and Mother tried their very best to draw him back. Mama cooked his favorite dishes when she could. She laid her hand on his arm, spoke softly.

But he only shook his head.

"I left you all alone," he whispered once. "I failed you."

Mama said fiercely, "You're here that is enough."

Father would wake up in the night reliving the darkest days he experienced in prison.

Mama would embrace him in her arms and sing until he fell back asleep.

As the weeks passed, Father's body began to fail him in small ways that accumulated like drops of rain in a bucket.

He started sleeping later, rising after the sun was already high. The fields, once his domain, became a place he watched from the doorway but rarely entered. His appetite came and went like the wind.

Some days were better than others. On good days, he would sit with us while we ate, ask about our lessons, even venture out to check on the oxen. These moments gave us hope.

But the bad days were getting worse. I would find him staring into the distance for hours, his thin cigarette burning down to his fingers without him noticing. His leg dragged more heavily. His cough, which had started as a minor irritation, began to sound deeper, more persistent.

"It's the wet season," Mama said when I asked about it. "The dampness gets into old injuries."

But we all knew it was more than that.

Then one evening Father surprised us by suggesting we sit

outside. It was a Fall night, the air was cool and clear, the first time in weeks without the oppressive humidity that made breathing difficult.

That night under the stars felt like a gift we didn't know we were receiving. It was the first time in two years that our family all sat together under the stars. I curled up on the porch under my father's arm, feeling how thin he'd become, but also feeling his warmth. He gazed up at the stars, his face bathed in silver light, silent, but peaceful.

"Look," he said, pointing to a cluster of stars. "The Seven Sisters. Your grandfather taught me those when I was your age."

Bo climbed onto his lap, and Father didn't wince with pain as he usually did. Even Khang sat closer than he had in weeks.

"Tell us about Grandfather," I said.

Father smiled—a real smile, not the careful one he'd been wearing for months. "He was a storyteller. He could make the stars dance with his words."

We sat there until the moon was high, listening to Father's voice grow stronger as he told us about his childhood, about our grandfather, about the way the world used to be.

When we finally went inside, I felt something I hadn't felt since his return—hope.

I should have known it was too good to last.

Three days later, Father could barely get out of bed.

It started with him sleeping through breakfast. When I went to wake him, his forehead was warm.

"Just tired," he mumbled, but his voice was weak, different.

By afternoon, he was shivering despite the heat. Mama brought him soup, but he could only manage a few spoonfuls before his stomach rebelled.

"It's nothing," he insisted, but we all heard the tremor in his voice.

That night, I lay awake listening to him cough. It was a wet, rattling sound that seemed to come from deep in his chest. Between coughing fits, I heard him whisper to Mama, "I'm sorry. I'm so sorry."

"For what?" she asked.

"For not being stronger. For not being the man, you married."

"You are," she said fiercely. "You are exactly the man I married."

But even in the darkness, I could hear her crying.

The sickness came in waves, fevers that scorched his skin one moment, and chills that left him unsteady the next.

Mama boiled herbs and laid cool cloths on his forehead. Khang and I took turns fanning him through the stifling nights.

But it was no use.

Malaria had found him—just as it had found so many in the low wet fields where mosquitoes swarmed.

At night, his coughing echoed through the house. Mama tried to make soup, crushed bitter roots, and begged him to eat. But he only grew weaker. The fevers always returning.

"It's just from the prison," Mama whispered to herself. "He needs rest."

But even I could see the sweat beading on his forehead, the quivering in his hands. Grandmother placed cool rags on his head and murmured prayers late into the night. I watched her lips move ceaselessly, begging old gods and new—anyone who would listen, to spare him.

Bed ridden and coughing throughout the nights he groaned about stomach pains, diarrhea, and vomiting. It was horrible to watch him struggle. Grandmother would sit at his bedside singing lullabies while Mother would try bathing and keeping him hydrated. The village doctor even came to make him more comfortable, giving him specialized herbs, but they did nothing.

The sickness settled into our house like an unwelcome guest who had no intention of leaving.

Some days, Father seemed almost normal. He would sit up in bed, ask about the rice harvest, even smile when Bo showed him a drawing. These moments became precious to us—we held them like precious coins.

But more often, he drifted in and out of fevered sleep. The malaria followed a pattern: chills that made him shake so violently the bed creaked, then burning fevers where sweat soaked through his clothes, then brief respites where he seemed almost like himself again.

Mama stayed beside him through the worst of it. Holding his hand during the trembling fits, and sang softly when he cried out for people who weren't there.

"Is he getting better?" I asked her one morning after a particularly long night.

Mama looked at me with tired eyes. "He's fighting," she said. "That's all we can ask."

But I saw how her hands shook when she thought no one was looking. I saw how she barely ate, how she prayed more fervently than ever before.

We were all fighting, but we were losing.

In his last week, Father seemed to understand what was coming. He called each of us to his bedside, speaking in a frail tone that we had to lean close to hear.

To Khang: "Take care of your mother and sisters. You're the man of the house now."

To me: "Keep reading. Keep learning. Education is the one thing they can never take from you."

To Bo: "Be good for your mama. Remember that your father loved you."

To Mama: "You were the best part of my life. Don't let this break you."

He gave me his book of poetry, pressing it into my hands with fingers that felt like twigs. "Read this when you miss me," he whispered. "I marked my favorite poems."

The night before he died, he was lucid for several hours. We all gathered around his bed, and he told us stories about his childhood, about the day he met Mama, about the dreams he'd had for us.

"I want you to remember me like this," he said. "Not sick. Not broken. Remember me loving you."

We promised we would.

We went to bed that night, believing Father still had more time.

But early that December morning, just as the first light touched the roof, he slipped away.

I was holding his hand when he died. It was thin and cold and still.

Mama cried out. Khang didn't speak, but held Bo who was whimpering and confused in his arms. Grandmother lit incense, her fingers shaking, and placed it near the altar, and prayed.

I sat there, still holding his hand, unable to process that the man who had taught me to read, who had carried me on his shoulders, who had filled our house with stories and laughter, was gone.

"He's at peace now," Grandmother said, but her voice shook.

Peace. The word felt foreign. How could there be peace in a world without my father?

I looked around the room at my family—at Mama bent over his body, at Khang trying to comfort Bo, at Grandmother preparing the ritual cloths—and felt a panic so complete it made my chest tight.

I had to get out. I had to run.

I had to find the one person who would understand that the world had just ended.

I ran.

I ran past the paddies, past the tall grasses, until I found myself standing across from Mai. She was selling sweet rice cakes with her mother, on the road to the city. She saw me coming—saw my face before I could speak—and dropped her basket.

"Minh," she said

I could not speak. Could not breathe.

I just grabbed her and held her as tight as I could while I sobbed. She held me while the world seemed to split beneath my feet. I thought of Father's voice reading to us by the oil lamp, his strong hands lifting Bo, the way he always kissed Mama's forehead before leaving. All of it gone in a night.

After what felt like hours in passing and having no more tears to weep, Mai walked me home.

"Do you want me to stay?" she asked at our gate.

I nodded, unable to speak.

She stayed with me the whole afternoon. That night, she even slept beside me on the mat and held my hand until morning.

When we woke, my home had been completely transformed. Neighbors had come and gone, bringing food, helping with preparations. Father's body had been washed and wrapped, incense burned steadily, and someone had covered the mirrors with cloth.

It looked like a house of mourning, but it didn't feel real. Part of me kept expecting to hear his cough from the back room, to see him shuffling to the kitchen for tea.

Mai stayed beside me through the rituals, through the endless stream of visitors. She even helped me eat when my stomach growled.

The next day the village gathered for the funeral. We laid Father to rest beneath the tamarind tree, where the earth was soft and the wind always found its way through the leaves. The monks chanted. Mama wept without sound.

Malaria, they said. But it was the prison that had killed him. The dampness, the cold, the beatings, the hunger—they had weakened him until even a mosquito could steal his life.

Later that week, I found one of Father's books tucked beneath his pillow. It was a thin volume of short stories, with his handwriting scrawled in the margins. I sat by the window and read every page. It smelled faintly of tobacco and ink. I traced the lines where his fingers must have held it, imagining him reading by candlelight. They were short stories he would tell us during mealtime, stories he used to entertain us, and now they were mine.

That evening, I told Mai about the book, and we lit a lantern by the porch. I read the short stories aloud while she sat beside me, her chin resting on her knees.

When I finished reading. I asked, "Do you remember when he carried me on his shoulders across the flooded path after the monsoon?"

Mai smiled. "You had your arms out like a bird. You thought you could fly."

I nodded, the memory blooming like jasmine in my chest. "I thought he was the tallest man in the world."

"He was," she said.

After, Mai returned each day. She helped Mama weed the garden, fed Bo when I couldn't, and braided my hair in the mornings.

She never asked for anything.

I learned then that grief has many forms, but so does love. Mai's quiet loyalty filled the space Father left behind. Not with noise or promises, but with presence.

The house felt different without him. Quieter. Dimmer. But we kept living. We planted new rice. We sang to Bo. We watched the sky change.

And we remembered.

Father was gone. But we remembered.

And in remembering, we held each other up.

CHAPTER 7

THE YEAR OF EMPTY BOWLS

In the months after Father's death, the seasons shifted.

The rains came late, and famine began with whispers—slow at first, then suffocating.

First, it was the neighbors—thin faces at the fence, asking if Mama had a handful of rice to spare. Then the markets grew quieter. No fish in the baskets. No chickens clucking in the cages. No sweet smell of roasted peanuts drifting through the air.

When the rains finally arrived, they were too heavy, washing away the young rice shoots before they could take hold. The river overflowed its banks, swallowing fields whole.

Then came a blistering drought. The stalks turned yellow and brittle under the ruthless sun. What little grain remained was seized by the colonial government for their own soldiers.

The market only carrying rice husks. There were no leftovers, no scraps.

The village, once full of music and laughter, grew silent. Even the Lantern Festival that year was canceled. I missed the warm glow of the river, the songs, the sweets. But most of all, I missed Father.

People began to disappear—not from war, but from hunger.

Mama did her best to hide a small stash of what rice she had, a clay jar buried beneath the floorboards, but even that would not last.

I woke each morning to the hollow ache of hunger gnawing at my belly. Khang grew thin and sharp-faced, his once bright eyes dulled. Little Bo cried weakly in his sleep, too small to understand the emptiness in his stomach.

We foraged for wild greens along the riverbank. We caught frogs, roasted dragonflies over tiny fires. Mama boiled thin soups that tasted only of water and salt.

Still, it was not enough.

I watched as proud families were reduced to begging at the roadside. Children with swollen bellies sat listlessly in the dirt. Others ate their pets and some simply walked into the river one night and did not return.

Khang would sit up at night wondering if Hooch was okay. He hadn't been around for some time to visit. And the villagers were eating any animal they could come across. Men with guns poached in the forest. Even when the game ran scarce, they would look under stones for worms to eat.

That year, Grandmother's fingers were swollen, her heart weak. She spent her days sitting on the porch, humming softly. Sometimes, if she had the strength, she braided my hair.

Mama boiled soup from river weeds and old fish bones. She dug for wild roots in the forest, trading what little cloth we had left for scraps of dried yam or millet.

By the time I was thirteen, my family had already boiled tree bark for broth, and chewed dried roots to calm the pangs in our bellies. The rains didn't improve. The paddies cracked. Even the ducks lay silent in the yard, too weak to waddle.

But death walked the roads openly now.

One morning, Grandmother didn't wake.

It was Mama who found her—still beneath the blanket, her hands crossed neatly over her chest, her mouth soft. There was no cry of panic. Only quiet.

I stood at the doorway, too stunned to move. Grandmother looked as if she were sleeping—dreaming, maybe, of rickshaws and mango trees and sons who came home.

The funeral was small. No procession, no drums. The famine still tore through the village. Everyone was burying someone— a grandfather, a mother, a baby who hadn't made it through the week.

Only our family stood there—Me, Khang, Mama, little Bo, Uncle Po, Aunt Tam, and my cousin Nguyet.

I placed a jasmine flower on Grandmother's chest.

"She loved you," Mama whispered. "You reminded her life could still be sweet."

I nodded, tears falling, remembering soft songs, sticky fingers, and the lap that had once held the whole world.

That night, I dreamed of her—Grandmother's voice, a lullaby without words, floating through the rice fields under the moonlight.

And for the first time in weeks, I slept without hunger in my belly.

But that was just a dream, the suffering was long from over.

Mai and I would go off digging for roots or trying to find anything edible. Then one sweltering afternoon, Mai and I passed the old Nguyen house, long abandoned since the patriarch died. In the yard stood, a lone mango tree, its leaves dull from thirst but still hanging on.

We stopped and stared at the branches.

All the ripe mangoes were gone—plucked by desperate hands weeks before.

But a few green ones still clung near the top, small and hard like clenched fists.

Mai's eyes narrowed.

"I can climb it."

I hesitated. "They're still sour."

"I don't care."

We returned at night, barefoot and silent. I climbed first, nimble from years of chasing chickens and climbing riverbanks. My fingers reached the lowest fruit, twisting it free.

We stole three that night. We didn't speak until we sat beneath the tree near Mai's home, each holding a mango like it was gold.

The flesh was stiff, bitter. But it filled our mouths.

Filling the silence in our bellies.

We went again the next evening. And the next.

Until the fourth night—when a voice cracked through the dark, "HEY! WHO'S THERE?!"

We froze.

Mr. Tam—the new owner of the Nguyen property—burst from the house, swinging a lantern, a heavy stick in his hand. His footsteps thundered over the dirt.

"RUN!" Mai hissed.

I hesitated. Mai, already in the tree, grabbed a mango, and hurled it at me. "GO!" she shouted.

So, I ran.

I glanced back once—just long enough to see her climbing back down. But by the time she reached the ground, we were already separated.

I didn't sleep that night. I kept replaying everything in my mind, terrified of what might've happened to her. I was so worried, I snuck out and crept toward her house to make sure she was all right.

Before I could reach her bedroom window, I heard her father shouting.

From inside, I could hear Mai's faint voice trembling. "But I was hungry..."

Uncle Hung roared back, "I'd rather we starve than steal! Do you have any idea how lucky you are that it was a neighbor who caught you—and not the soldiers?"

His voice rose, sharp and cruel. "Did you see what they did to that boy who stole?"

A few days earlier, a young boy had been caught by the French stealing a loaf of bread. They tied him to the village well and beat his hands with wooden batons until his fingers shattered. It was meant as a lesson to all of us—a warning of what happened to thieves.

I was truly afraid of the French. They could imprison you without reason, humiliate you in the streets, beat you senseless, even execute you—simply for being in the wrong place at the wrong time. No one was safe.

Inside, Mai's father towered over her—a leather belt in hand. Her mother wept quietly in the corner.

Screams rang out as Mai shouted in pain.

The count of twenty lashes.

She lay face down on a straw mat, her back raw and blistered.

Even turning her head sent shivers of pain through her spine.

I snuck in after her parents fell asleep. I carried a wet cloth with me, dipped in cool water to ease the stings and welts forming on her back.

As Mai cried in pain, I held her hand to comfort her. Then I reached into my bag, "I brought you something."

Pulling out a single mango we stole from the tree that night, wrapped in a banana leaf.

Green. Under ripened. Bitter.

I peeled it with shaking hands and lifted a slice to Mai's mouth.

Mai opened her lips and bit gently. Sucking as much juice as she could out of it. Her face twisted—puckered by the sourness—but then, to my surprise, she smiled.

"This…" she whispered, her voice hoarse, "this is the sweetest mango I've ever tasted."

My eyes welled.

Mai sucked the juice slowly, lips sticky. "You were worth it, mango," she whispered, laughing through her pain.

I laughed, too. Quietly at first, then louder, until we both laid side by side, our ribs aching from laughter, not hunger.

And for the second time that year I felt that I wasn't starving.

We were full—with friendship, with loyalty, with a love stronger than our pain.

After that day, Mai and I never stole again. Mr. Tam's mangos had kept us alive, but we feared Mai's father more than we feared going hungry. One warning was all we'd get—if he caught us again, it wouldn't just be a lashing. He might just beat us to death. But I was grateful to Uncle Hung, he never mentioned a word of my misdeeds to my mother.

As the famine continued, my Mama gave us smaller and smaller portions, just a few mouthfuls of rice porridge. Mother would pretend she had already eaten, but her protruding cheekbones and sunken eyes said otherwise. Khang would lick his bowl clean after every meal, hoping for one last grain of rice.

We all tried to pretend it would pass, but when I looked at my family, really looked, I saw ribs, collarbones, and veins that should have been hidden by flesh: now too visible under our translucent skin. That's how skinny we had become. The hunger had hollowed us out, dulling even the ache in our bellies. We no longer craved food—not because we were full, but because our bodies had forgotten how it felt to eat.

Then, Bo got sick.

Mother didn't know what to do. We were all already on the brink of death and so many children in the village had already died from starvation. The days were growing more desperate. Those who had anything left weren't sharing—and most, if asked, had nothing to give.

That afternoon, Ma left the house. She went door to door, begging the neighbors for anything they could spare. She came home empty-handed.

The next evening, as Bo's weak cries echoed through the house and the air thickened with heat and sorrow, we had given up hope. Mother wrapped Bo in a blanket, rocking him in her arms, she looked Khang and I in the eyes and told us we need to prepare for the worst, and that our little brother could die.

Then there was a knock at the door.

It was Mai.

She stood quietly in the doorway, holding a small basket wrapped carefully in cloth. Inside were thin strips of dried fish, a single egg, and a bit of meat—small but precious, like treasure.

I stared in disbelief, my mouth watering.

"My father said to bring this," Mai said softly. "He couldn't give it to you himself—too many prying eyes."

Mama's hands trembled as she took the basket. For a long moment, she said nothing.

Then she dropped to her knees and pulled Mai into her arms, tears streaming down her face.

"Thank you," she whispered, voice breaking. "Thank you, child."

With the food Mai's family shared, Bo's condition slowly improved. Soon his cries softened and he would smile when I played with him.

Every morning, Mai left whatever scraps her family could spare: meat bones, wilted vegetables, a hand-size of rice. They were starving themselves but shared what little they had. Without them, Bo would have surely died.

As days passed, our condition became stable. Uncle Po visited Mama, he didn't know how bad our situation was and immediately gave us the rice balls he carried in his pocket.

The next day Uncle returned with more food, and it filled our bellies so fast we actually got belly aches from eating too quickly.

Finally, we felt relieved and comforted by Uncle Po's and Mai's family's generosity, giving us a renewed sense of hope.

But Uncle Po didn't just bring rice, he brought news. "It's beginning," he said. "We can't be silent forever."

As the famine continued, the city and villagers grew restless. That week, something shifted in the people, they stopped fearing the French, and organized to resist them

A group of men and women gathered in the square, holding white signs painted with shaky black letters—Freedom for Vietnam, No More Taxes, End the Occupation. They shouted slogans through cupped hands, their voices rising in waves of anger and hope. I had never seen so many people shouting in unison, "Our country, Our Freedom" and "Vietnam for the Vietnamese."

Mama pulled me back toward the alley, but I saw it all.

The French soldiers arrived in formation, rifles slung over their backs, batons in hand, and leashed dogs. Without warning, they marched into the crowd. The air turned sharp with panic. I watched as peaceful chants became shrieks. The batons were swung across backs, shoulders, and arms raised in defense. A woman fell to the ground clutching her child.

Then a protester threw a rock.

Then another.

A barrage of rocks were flung at the French.

Then a glass bottle ignited in the air—flames bursting at a soldier's feet. The French fired back. I heard the crack of gunfire, and three people fell to the ground, clutching where the bullets entered their bodies, they did not rise again.

Afterward, the market shut down. The French posted guards at every entrance. No one came or left without being searched. At night, we heard boots outside. Men were taken from their homes—for questioning. Even the villagers weren't spared from accusations.

Ma forbid me from going back to the market after the riot, so Mai and I were left to only play in the village.

And as the famine slowly improved, Mai and I would spend long afternoons sitting together beneath the stilted houses, whispering dreams of better days. My cousin Nguyet, three years younger, often joined us. Mai spoke of traveling the world, maybe opening her own shop. She said she would date many boys and never settle down.

I, on the other hand, imagined marrying a farmer like my father and living in the countryside.

Nguyet didn't yet like boys and would say we were strange. Mai and I would laugh and tell her, "Just you wait."

Each day the three of us grew closer, but Mai and I grew more attached than ever.

We sat by the dry streambed, watching dragonflies buzz over the cracked mud. Sometimes I brought a few scraps of charcoal, and we drew on flat stones: pictures of steaming bowls of rice, roast duck, bananas, soft cakes shaped like moons.

"Someday," Mai whispered, "we'll eat like queens."

I smiled. "Someday we'll be queens."

The famine lasted nearly a year.

When the rains returned, when rice seedlings finally stood straight in the paddies again, when food began trickling back into the markets—it was as if the village exhaled all at once.

But not all had survived to see it.

More than a million had died across the country.

I never forgot the quiet graves dug at the edge of the forest— nameless mounds marked with sticks and pieces of cloth.

But my family survived.

The famine lifted.

And life, in slow stubborn steps, began again.

CHAPTER 8

RICE GIRLS OF THE MARKET

The revolt failed, but something shifted. Perhaps it was guilt, or fear, or politics. Whatever the reason, the French began reviewing their policies. Taxes were lowered. Soldiers stationed near our village no longer kicked down doors or dragged men away in the night. Some even smiled in the market. One officer handed out sweets to children. Another offered to help fix a neighbor's broken cart wheel.

But I didn't trust their smiles. Not after what they did to Father. A sugar cube couldn't wash away blood.

Still, people began to live again.

The fields filled with color. Ducks waddled through the irrigation ditches. We heard singing from the market stalls. My family farmed again, and with the rains and good seed, the paddies flourished.

Khang, now the eldest man of our house, stepped into Father's shoes without complaint. He rose before dawn, hauling the cart out to the fields with Mama. His shoulders growing broader each week. By midday, his shirt clung to his back, soaked with sweat as he lifted heavy sacks onto the ox cart. Bo followed him everywhere, trying to mimic his swing with a stick. I would sometimes catch Mama watching Khang with a mix of pride and sadness—her son now carrying the weight of a man's world.

Now old enough to carry a sickle, I walked the rows beside Khang, the sun on our backs, our blades slicing in rhythm. Even Bo had grown skilled with the finger knife, stripping the husks with surprising speed. When evening came, we returned tired but full of something we hadn't felt in a long time—hope.

With the harvests good and the market paying well, Khang took over selling in town. Mama said her feet had worked enough for a lifetime, she continued to work the fields but trusted Khang to sell at the market. In the evenings she stayed home to tend the garden and rest in the shade. We saved coins in a tin hidden under a loose floorboard. Some nights, Mama even made sweet rice with coconut milk, and we'd eat slowly, savoring each bite.

But my favorite moments came after the rice was picked and Khang had gone off to market. That's when I would run down to meet Mai and Nguyet by the tamarind tree, where the other children waited with jump ropes, sticks, and laughter. And then Hooch appeared. We hadn't seen him since the famine but he looked healthy, I knew Khang would be pleased to know he was okay.

We played hopscotch on the dusty path behind the shrine, using stones for markers. Nguyet always drew the squares crooked, but she skipped like a deer and rarely lost. We made ropes from old fishing twine, jumping until our legs gave out. I taught Bo how to spin while he jumped, and he beamed with pride when he finally managed two full spins without falling.

Our favorite was Dragon-Snake. We stood in a line, arms wrapped around each other's waists, the first child acting as the head of the snake, the last as the tail. A "doctor" chased us, trying to split the chain. If the snake broke, the doctor took the place in the link of the chain where it was broken and the next person would become the doctor. We'd laugh and scream, falling into the grass in tangled heaps.

Nguyet loved Blind Man's Bluff. We tied an old cloth around the seeker's eyes and scattered through the courtyard, calling, "Over here!" and darting away before being caught. She had the best hiding spot—behind the half-broken altar at the shrine, where incense ashes still clung to the stone.

The shrine had other secrets, too.

When the sun began to set and the sky turned gold, Mai would creep behind the shrine wall and wail like a ghost. She made her voice echo through the stone, sending Nguyet shrieking toward the rice paddies. "You're cruel!" Nguyet would cry, but we couldn't stop laughing.

Sometimes we pretended the shrine was haunted. We'd creep around its mossy stones, whispering tales of ghost brides and soldiers who never left the war. We made talismans from banana leaves and performed mock rituals to "appease" the spirits. Once, we covered ourselves in white cloth, arms outstretched, chasing each other through the dusk with ghostly moans. Our laughter rang out across the fields.

Nguyet clutched her banana leaf talisman like it could really keep the ghosts away. She still believed in fairy tales, but sometimes her eyes hinted she knew they weren't real. That was the thing about growing up in our village—magic faded fast, but it never vanished entirely.

When we grew tired of ghosts, we would play fetch with Hooch, tossing him a stick, which he always retrieved. Hooch loved to play around Mai almost as much as Khang, since she often brought him snacks that her mother Lianne cooked the night before. Even the stray was able to taste the best food in town.

Those were the days I cherished most with Mai. The days where sorrow stayed quiet and joy was loud again.

Still, sometimes Mai would vanish. I'd find her crouched at the edge of the field path, her chin resting in her hand, eyes fixed on something—or someone.

It didn't take long to realize who.

She watched Khang. Watched him sling the sacks of rice onto the cart like they were feathers. Watched the way his muscles rippled with each motion, the way the sunlight glistened off his shoulders. She didn't say a word about it, but I saw how pink her cheeks turned when he smiled in her direction.

"Why aren't you playing?" I asked once, catching her by surprise.

"I am," she replied, not turning her gaze. "Just a different kind of game."

I didn't know what that meant then. But I would, someday.

Nguyet, still too young to care for anything other than sweets and winning races, rolled her eyes and dragged Mai back to the games.

But I noticed the way Mai lingered a little longer at our house in the evenings. The way she helped Mama chop vegetables, the way she always asked where Khang had gone if he wasn't home.

Sometimes, I didn't mind that Mai liked Khang. But I did mind that when he came around, she forgot we were telling a story, or that I was even there.

Things were changing.

We were growing older, all of us. Our games grew shorter, and our chores longer. But laughter still echoed through the trees, and we still ran barefoot under the sun.

I laughed, louder than I meant to. And then I felt it—that quick sting in my chest, like I'd betrayed my father by forgetting for a moment that he passed.

For now, the market was full, the fields were green, and the rice girls still played.

Even if the world beyond the village whispered new things.

Our footsteps, marched toward something we couldn't yet see.

CHAPTER 9

THE AGE OF WORKING

When Mai and I turned fourteen, we began going to the market with Khang.

The Hue market was a storm of sound and scent. Cloth canopies flapped overhead, casting moving shadows on crates of sugarcane, heaps of chili peppers, and baskets of dried shrimp. Merchants hollered, their voices stacking like waves.

"Salt! Pure as the sea!"

"Get your eels here! Fresh from the delta!"

A woman sold lychees from a wheelbarrow, her baby strapped to her back, asleep through the noise. A man roasted quail eggs over open coals, the smell curling like incense. Next to him, a group of girls wove flower crowns and pinned them in one another's hair for tips.

Each day followed the same rhythm—the lifting, the laughter, the songs we hummed as we scooped rice into leaf-wrapped bundles. Under a canopy of patched umbrellas, we shouted, "Rice for sale! Get your rice here!" Our voices rose above the chatter of the morning crowd.

Our arms toned from carrying the heavy sacks and our throats sharpened from shouting prices.

Khang would shake his head and laugh. "You're scaring them off. Try smiling instead."

We did. And sometimes it worked.

We called ourselves the rice girls—and people remembered us.

Two years passed like a warm breeze, and suddenly we were sixteen.

It was around this time that Mai began acting differently. She took extra care with her braids, checking their neatness in the reflection of a tin bowl. Her voice grew softer—almost floated when she spoke. In the evenings, she helped my mother stir soup and slice herbs, always asking, "Where's Khang?"

I knew she liked him, but this crush had gone on long enough.

At first, I tried to ignore it. But the way her eyes tracked him as he moved through the house, the way she lingered by the front gate when he came back from the fields—it was impossible to miss.

One afternoon, I caught her trying to flirt. She leaned awkwardly against the cabinet in the most unnatural yet inviting way, arching her back to accentuate whatever curves she thinks she had, and asked Khang if he could help her stir the rice.

I was in the doorway drinking goat milk and laughed so hard it shot out my nose. Mai's face went crimson. I couldn't stop pointing at her, cackling. Khang just looked puzzled, like the whole thing had gone right over his head. Mai stormed off, furious.

"You're too funny," I called after her.

She turned, blinking. "I am?"

"He's my brother," I said.

"So?" she replied, grinning. "He's strong. And kind. Doesn't that count for something?"

I didn't know what to say. It felt strange—like two parts of my life were crossing lines they weren't meant to.

I simply laughed and said, "I didn't know you wanted to be my sister-in-law that bad."

We both ended up laughing about it and made up on the spot.

Later that week, while folding tarps at dusk, I brought it up to Khang.

"Mai likes you," I said.

He frowned. "Mai? She's a kid. It's just a phase. She doesn't even know what she wants."

"She's our age."

He shrugged. "Exactly. Still a kid."

I got frustrated at him, "She's too good for you anyway," I snapped, and stormed off before he could say anything.

I didn't even know why I said it. It's not like I wanted them to be together. But somehow, I still felt the need to defend her.

I never told Mai what Khang said. But I watched her more closely after that. She still smiled when he walked by, but something in her eyes dimmed.

It was in that quiet gap between girlhood and something else that we first noticed Vinh.

He worked across the road, at the furniture stall nestled between clay pots and woven baskets. He was our age, tall and tan, with arms toned from lifting carved chairs and polished tables. When he laughed, a single dimple formed on his left cheek.

Mai noticed him first.

"I think his smile could sell a thousand chairs," she whispered behind her hand.

"You'd buy one just to sit closer," I teased.

We giggled, peeking at him between hanging tarps, stealing glances like children sneaking mangoes.

When he wiped sweat from his brow and looked up, our eyes met. We turned away fast, our faces burning like chilies in the sun.

Each day after that, we made excuses to look his way.

"I think he looked at you today," Mai would say.

"No," I'd reply, "he was looking at you."

This game lasted weeks.

Then one morning, he crossed the street.

Mai dropped the bamboo spoon in her hand, and my heartbeat stumbled.

"Hello," Vinh said warmly.

We froze.

Khang appeared behind us, wiping his hands. "Hey! Looking to buy some rice?"

"I'll take two pounds," Vinh replied, though his gaze had already found us. It lingered on Mai just a little longer.

As Khang scooped the rice, Vinh smiled. "I see you here every morning. You two work hard."

"Thank you," Mai whispered, her voice like silk.

I didn't know what to say. I stared at my hands and noticed a grain of rice under my fingernail.

Vinh leaned in, "I hear you sell the best rice in the market. Can't wait to try it."

Vinh leaned back casually and confident, my brother handed him the rice, Vinh said, "I'll see you later" and he swiftly crossed the street back to his shop.

I looked over at Mai, stunned by what had just happened. Her ears turned bright pink. She gave me a shy laugh.

"Did that really just happen?"

Khang laughed. "You've got a crush on Vinh."

"I do not."

He raised an eyebrow. "I meant Mai. Wait—do you?"

"I do not," I said again, too quickly.

Vinh started visiting more. Sometimes for rice. Sometimes for nothing in particular.

Khang's friends—Kiet and Beni—noticed, too.

"Careful, sis," Beni teased. "You'll forget how to sell rice and just hand it out to cute boys."

Kiet shouted across the road, "Hey, Vinh, want me to ask the rice girls out for you?"

"Which one is your favorite," huh?

"Don't eat too much rice Vinh you might get fat and they won't like you anymore."

Vinh was unbothered by their teasing.

Mai and I tried to laugh along. We told ourselves it's just harmless, boys being boys.

One day Mai stayed home to help her mother cook. Vinh came over, noticed she was missing.

"Where's your friend today?" I noticed Vinh sounded differently that day, his voice seemed more friendly and less flirtatious.

"Home," I said.

His smile softened. "Tell her I said hi."

That night, Mai showed up at my door. "Did you see Vinh today?"

"He asked about you," I replied.

She blushed.

The next few days, they grew closer. I noticed the way Vinh's eyes brightened when she arrived. I noticed she stopped waiting for me before walking to market. She crossed the road once to see him—just walked right over and didn't look back.

Later, she gave him mung bean cakes wrapped in banana leaves.

"He's nice, isn't he?" she asked.

"He's fine," I said.

"Did I say something wrong?"

"No," I lied. "Just tired."

One day in the market Khang was annoyed by Mai and I, he asked us to go shopping and said he would watch the stall himself. So, we took off immediately, walking the length of the market, listening and watching, wondering what we could do for entertainment.

Then we saw them—old bicycles propped near a tool shed stall. Rusty, but still functional. Vinh, the furniture seller's son, had been repairing them with parts he collected from traders. He had two nearly working.

He grinned when he saw us. "Want to ride?" he asked, offering the taller one to Mai.

We hesitated. Girls weren't usually seen biking—especially not to the old rice mill. But we wanted to see everything.

So, we said yes.

That day riding the bikes became like a secret escape. We went down dusty roads, biked trails in the forest, and ended our trip at an abandoned rice mill, where old rebel flags once hung. Hooch was there laying in the grass under the sweltering sun.

"So is this where you sleep?" I asked.

We pet him for a while, then played a cat and mouse game dodging and weaving between the trees as he chased us. After awhile he got bored of us and trailed off back into the forest. We never knew where he slept at night, Hooch would always disappear before dark, but we assumed he may have been a rebel dog in the fight against the French, since we found him near their base.

When we returned our bikes to Vinh he gave Mai a wooden charm in the shape of a lotus flower.

"My father made extras, but I only have one," he said. "Thought you might like it."

Mai's eyes widened, "For me?" she gasped.

He grinned. "Unless you two want to fight for it."

Mai giggled. I didn't.

Although I was upset that Vinh took a liking to Mai I wasn't going to let a boy come between us.

As Mai and I walked back to my brother Khang, we came across a jewelry stall. All the items looked cheaply made and of poor quality. But then my eyes fell upon two matching lockets. Dainty but strong, I thought this would be a perfect gift for sisters to share.

I asked how much.

The lady at the stall smiled brightly. "You've made a very good choice," she said. "This is a beautiful necklace. Tell you what—take the pair for a pound of rice."

"Sold!" I shouted without hesitation.

For the first time, Mai and I had something that was truly ours—matching necklaces to mark our friendship, strong and lasting. We wore them with pride, fingers constantly brushing against the pendants to make sure they were still there. We checked them so often, it became a habit—out of fear more than vanity. We were terrified of losing them.

Every day, those necklaces reminded us—we had each other. And that meant something.

The Hue Festival was approaching. A grand celebration of our imperial history. This year, we were old enough to attend on our own. It was an event only celebrated every two years to celebrate Vietnam's former imperial capitol.

Mai and I began preparing.

We decorated fans, tried on dresses. We even bought make-up—just a little—with money saved from rice sales.

Vinh, who we grew rather fond of from letting us use his bikes, invited us to meet him at his shop in the heart of the city.

We took him up on his offer because it was in the dead center of town where the parade would take place.

I wore my best *ao dài*, deep blue with white embroidery at the hem, my long black hair tired in a loose knot. My skin was tan, my hands rough from harvests, and my shoulders lean and strong from years of carrying baskets of rice. Mai tied her hair with a crimson ribbon. Her skin was fairer than mine, she walked softly and looked delicate.

The city bloomed with spectacular lights and lanterns. Silk dragons writhed through the narrow streets, carried by children in masks. Music floated like perfume through the streets. Red and gold paper fluttered above the market square like leaves in a warm wind. The night shimmered.

Mai and I walked together through the crowd, arms brushing now and then. We saw Vinh waiting outside the shop for us. He looked so handsome with his combed hair, slacks, and button-down shirt.

When he saw us, he smiled and said, "You came! Wow you look stunning."

My heart fluttered, but Vinh looked past me. His eyes settled on Mai. Her body more supple, her face like a porcelain doll.

We walked together through the festival—the three of us—eating candied fruit and seeing children play in the distance. Couples walked hand in hand.

We sat near the square where people danced and cheered. The parade would begin soon and we had the perfect view.

Then Vinh asked Mai if she wanted a drink. She nodded and they stood up together. She looked at me and said, "I'll be right back." Then they disappeared into the crowd, while I waited for them to return.

Then Kiet and Beni arrived, both of them gasping when they saw my dress.

Embarrassed, I smoothed the fabric over my hips and tucked a loose strand of hair behind my ear.

"Well look at you," Kiet said, grinning. "You really clean up nice for a rice girl."

Beni elbowed him. "So, where's Mai? Did you come alone?"

I smiled. "I'm just waiting for her and Vinh. They went off to get a drink."

"More like a smooch," Kiet snorted.

They both started whistling and cracking more jokes, nudging each other like mischievous schoolboys.

Kiet always knew how to make people laugh, even when there was nothing funny.

Beni had always followed Kiet, like my younger brother Bo always mimicking Khang.

He looked up to him—not just for his banter and laughs, but for the way Kiet could make others feel.

As cunning as Kiet was with his words, he was the kind of boy who would carry someone else's bucket if theirs was too heavy, without saying a word.

Those two reminded me so much of myself and Mai.

Ten minutes had passed. Then twenty. The parade began and I was slightly distracted watching the events unfold.

Soon an hour had passed, Mai and Vinh nowhere to be seen. The parade was over, the lanterns burned low. As the lights dimmed, the moon rose higher in the sky, the crowd thinned and the streets emptied.

Kiet and Beni left, saying they were heading home.

When Mai returned, her cheeks were flush and eyes shining. She reached for my hand, "I need to tell you something."

Mai smiled, nervous and glowing. "Vinh asked me to be his girlfriend, and I accepted."

I stood silent, the sound of a distant drum echoed faintly in the night.

I smiled, too wide. "Congratulations."

She studied my face. "You're not mad?"

"Why would I be?"

And I meant it. At least, I wanted to. How could I not be happy for my friend?

But afterward, everything changed.

In the weeks that followed, Mai still came with me to the market, but her heart was somewhere else. We used to laugh and gossip while we sold our rice. Now, her eyes often wandered down the road, waiting for a glimpse of Vinh. She started leaving earlier, returning late, humming little melodies under her breath.

One day, after we packed up our baskets, she turned to me and said, "One day, I'm going to marry Vinh."

I blinked. "What?"

She giggled, then looked serious. "He's perfect."

"I'm glad he makes you happy," I said.

In my head I was thinking, *When am I going to find myself a boy?*

She smiled dreamily. "I swear we're in love."

"Well, I wish you two the best of luck."

But inside, a tiny voice whispered, *And what about me?*

More time passed. We turned seventeen.

One day, down by the river, Mai braided my hair. Her fingers moved gently, twisting strands into place.

Then, in the quietest voice, she asked, "Do you know...how to make love?"

I stared at the water, not answering right away.

My mouth opened wide, "What kind of question is that?"

"You know. How it works. What it's like," said Mai.

I shrugged, unsure whether to be honest or cautious. "No. But I've heard stories. Why?"

She blushed and looked down. "No reason. Just curious."

But she wasn't just curious. I could see it in her smile; in the way she touched her own wrist absently when she spoke of him. There was something blooming in her—something new.

As annoying as it was, I still couldn't deny that Vinh made Mai happy. She moved through the world now with lightness in her step.

One day, Vinh's store was closed, his father out of town on business. Yet Vinh still had a key, and he asked Mai to join him to rearrange some things his father asked of him in his absence.

Overjoyed Mai took his hand and off they went.

Later she returned, her hair unbraided. I clearly remember braiding it the day before. She said nothing, but her cheeks were cherry red.

I suspected something was up and asked, "Did something happen?"

Mai looked down acting coy and swaying side to side, "No."

As Mai became more absent in the market the neighborhood kids started sharing rumors with me that Vinh and Mai would sneak off on his bikes and ride down to the old abandoned rice mill.

The one Mai and I found the day we took Vinh's bikes for our ride together.

I grabbed Kiet's shirt twisting his neck collar in my fist and said, "Don't you ever lie about my friend again."

His face turned as red as a tomato, squirming in fear he said, "I'm sorry, it was just a joke."

But I questioned if it was a joke. Mai returned, I never asked her, never told her about the rumors I had heard, and she never told me about what happened between her and Vinh on their walks.

Summer came, and with it, long days at the market.

Soon it felt like Mai and Vinh were inseparable. On occasions, he even came to my family's rice fields to walk with us to the market. He would carry Mai's bag as if it were nothing.

One day in the field looking out at the rolling hills, Mai looked at me and said, "I want to give my whole self to Vinh."

I asked, "What does that mean?"

She didn't answer. She just looked back out scanning the rice paddies with her eyes.

I didn't press her. Some things aren't meant to be explained—only felt.

That evening, after the market emptied and the light began to fade, I walked down to the river alone.

I didn't tell Mama or Mai. I needed a moment—not because anything was wrong, but because something inside me felt like it was shifting.

The water moved slow, heavy with silt and stories. It had carried our lanterns on festival nights, our prayers and laughter and whispered dreams. But now, it was quiet. Just the sound of insects in the grass and the occasional splash of a frog leaping from the reeds.

I slipped off my sandals and stepped into the shallows. The mud clung to my toes, cool and familiar. Across the current, the far bank was shadowed, but I could still see the outline of the tamarind tree where Mai and I had made our promises as children.

I remembered that night so clearly—our lanterns bobbing down this very stretch of river, our wishes sent off into the dark.

Please let Mai and I stay together, always.

I whispered the words again, though I wasn't sure if I still believed them. People changed. We were changing. Mai laughed more softly now, and watched Vinh with eyes I didn't understand. I no longer climbed trees or chased butterflies. I carried sacks, counted coins, planned harvests.

Was this what growing up felt like? Like standing in a river that kept moving, even when you wanted it to stand still?

I crouched and dipped my hand into the water. It slipped through my fingers like silk. For a moment, I wished Father were here. I would've asked him what to do when joy started to feel like something you had to protect.

I picked up a stone—round and smooth—and turned it over in my palm. Then, without thinking, I whispered, "Please let us all find our way," and tossed it into the current.

It made no sound. Just a ripple that spread, then vanished.

I walked back, barefoot and steadier, knowing nothing had changed—and yet somehow, everything had.

The river kept flowing. And we kept growing up.

CHAPTER 10

THE NEW OPPRESSOR

On September 22nd of 1940, Japan would station troops in Vietnam. Japan quickly gained control of key French bases.

The war had reached the capital. French soldiers had vanished, chased into retreat by an occupying force of the Japanese.

For a while the villagers cheered, independence seemed to arrive as the French colonizers fled. Those locked in French detention centers like my father were released. Families reunited, and the fall of colonial rule over our people had ended.

For months Mai and I felt more safe and secure under the Japanese occupation than we ever did during French rule. Rice taxes had been lifted, and our dealings in the market were simpler without soldiers monitoring us.

Sales in the market were up, we couldn't produce rice fast enough, many soldiers at the market would visit Mai and I and buy up all our rice.

I was seventeen now.

I had matured into a grown woman, my hands strong and hardened by years of fieldwork. My cheeks still held the roundness of girlhood, but my eyes no longer shimmered with the lightness of childhood. They had grown dark—haunted, even before the worst came.

Across the dirt path, Mai had fully bloomed. Her face was still soft and kind, but it carried something sharper now—a new awareness, a heaviness she never used to have.

My mother and older brother Khang decided that since Mai and I could make our journey to the market on our own, they could pick additional rice in the evening, essentially bringing in more yield.

But soon we learned the Japanese who we revered as our saviors were still our oppressors. Sleek and silent in pressed uniforms and black boots they marched. Their language was foreign, but their power was the same—rifles, orders, fear.

By 1943, our Japanese allies needed supplies to fund their war. They would strip the lands, taking everything that was left to feed their military.

Even though we lived in fear of the Japanese, we still rose before dawn. We farmed what we could. We still rode the ox cart to the market, selling our goods. Survival became a ritual, and the rituals kept us sane.

My brother Khang was twenty now, a man by all accounts. He looked so much like our father that sometimes, when the light hit him just right, my mother's breath would catch. He worked the fields late into the afternoon and always walked to the market in the evening to take Mai and me home.

Vinh was older, still selling furniture for his father, but his voice had grown deeper, steadier—like a drumbeat beneath the chaos. There were days he and Mai exchanged glances longer than necessary, and I began to notice the invisible threads that tethered them together, delicate but undeniable.

Still, we produced more than ever that year, but all good things come to an end.

The city would be ransacked, no stone unturned to find food. At the market, the Japanese would take 80% of our rice and only let us sell the other 20.

Not even our small village was spared.

One day they came to our village to "collect for the army."

Mai's father had been preparing for the army's visit. On the day the Japanese soldiers entered our village, Uncle Hung told us to take some livestock and hide in the woods. "Take the black chicken and the white goat. Go to the cave near the waterfall. Don't come back unless I come for you. Do you understand?"

Every animal that remained, every bag of feed, was taken. They left no food and no payment.

Mai's father tried to resist.

He begged they leave his animals alone. Once Mai and I hid the goat and chicken where they wouldn't be discovered Mai insisted on returning to the village. She was deeply concerned for what the Japanese might do if her father was discovered for withholding from the army.

When we got back, we saw people being dragged out of their homes and pushed on the ground near the village well.

The villagers were scared, people's hands were folded together in prayer, and families clung to their loved ones. Soldiers pointed their rifles at them.

I walked over to my mother and brothers and sat down next to them. Mother looked at me with fear and disbelief as to why I returned.

As Mai walked over to sit by her mother, one of the soldiers eyed up Mai, and said something, reaching out and touching her hair. The other soldiers laughed.

Mai's father, enraged by the glance the soldier gave, began shouting at the Japanese. The soldier slapped Mai's father in the face and a scuffle ensued. Mai's father grabbed the soldier by the throat and threw him to the ground, pressing a knee to his chest, choking him with all his strength.

The other soldiers shouted trying to pull Mai's father off their friend, but Mai's dad was strong, and they couldn't pry the soldier from her father's grasp. A senior officer swung his rifle like a club, cracking the back of Hung's skull. He collapsed, unconscious, blood spilling out of the back of his head onto the soil.

My heart was pounding; I lept forward to stand up and run to Mai but my mother clung tightly to my hand and pulled me back down. Mother shook her head, "no," meaning she didn't want me to intervene. She was probably right, me rushing to embrace Mai would have caused more harm than good.

The soldier who was being choked gathered his bearings. He stood up and began kicking Mai's father, shouting obscenities. The senior officer shouted for his men to restrain the soldier.

The captain of the troops, tucked in his uniform which became undone in the struggle, and read a thank you letter in Vietnamese to the villagers.

It read:

> *Thank you for supporting our efforts to keep Vietnam free from the Western countries. Japan is here to protect and liberate Vietnam. Together we will achieve success and unite all of Asia. Thank you for your sacrifice and your loyalty to the emperor.*

He looked to his men, and whistled loudly. The soldiers began packing the things they had taken, backed away, and disappeared back into the jungle.

Mai and her mother quickly ran to Mai's father. He had a gash in his head but he was conscious and talking. They quickly helped him into his home. Mother grabbed bandages and we went over to help. Mai's father asked, "Did you hide the hen and goat?"

Mai replied, "Yes."

Her father said, "Good."

Mai with tears in her eyes apologized, "I'm sorry father, I should have listened and stayed hidden."

Mai's father looked up at her as her mother tightened the final bandage on his head and said, "Don't worry, what happened was not your fault, I'm just glad my little girl is safe."

My brother Khang would be sent in the night to retrieve the goat and hen so they wouldn't be killed in the night by some wild animal.

I waited up until he returned, but as soon as he came home and I knew he was safe, my emotions and exhaustion made me collapse, falling into a deep sleep.

I dreamed of my father being beaten in prison, my grandmother starving, and now it haunted me to see Mai's father being struck over the head with a gun.

The next morning when I woke from my nightmare I saw Mai's father outside his hut at work. He was milking the goat and the hen already laid a fresh egg.

Mai's mother was already churning the fresh milk into a rough, salty cheese.

The food was meager, but it kept them fed.

CHAPTER 11

BENEATH THE BLOSSOMS, SECRETS BLOOM

For a while it felt like the famine had returned. People struggled since the army took so much, but the land was healthy and prospering, so no one starved.

Mai and I learned how to be friendlier in the market, and flirt with the soldiers who oftentimes loosened their pockets and gave us a few extra yen, which had a greater currency than our own.

Then on a summer day, after a long morning of picking and packing, Khang bid us farewell as Mai and I headed to the market. My little brother Bo, now thirteen, tugged at my sleeve and asked if he could come with us.

"Bo, *mẹ sẽ đợi em ở nhà,*" I said gently. Mother will be waiting for you.

But Bo pleaded and insisted, his eyes bright with excitement. "Please, just this once! I want to see the city, to help!"

Mai touched my arm. "Why don't you let him come?" she said. "He's strong now and could help us unload."

I hesitated.

Bo was still a boy, but lately he'd grown into his limbs, his voice cracking in awkward bursts. He wanted so badly to be seen as a man. I looked at Mai, then back at Bo.

"Fine," I said. "But you must stay close."

We let Khang know, in case Mother came looking. Then we packed the cart with baskets of rice, dried beans, and small jars of chili paste. Bo rode in the back, straddling a sack of rice, his eyes wide with anticipation. He looked like a puppy, so eager to be useful, so proud to be included.

It was an ordinary day.

Until it wasn't.

The checkpoint was sudden.

Japanese soldiers stepped out of the trees just as the cart crossed the old bridge.

They shouted in a language we didn't understand, rifles raised.

I froze.

Mai tried to smile, to bow respectfully. But they weren't looking for respect.

One of the soldiers grabbed me by the arm and dragged me from the cart. Another pulled Mai down. Their hands were rough. Their breaths smelled of old tobacco and something sour. Their eyes were empty.

They did not spare either of us that day—Mai and I were both taken, brutalized in the dirt while others mocked us in laughter.

Bo screamed.

He ran toward them, fists flying. "Don't hurt them! Don't hurt my sister!"

One of the soldiers turned and, without hesitation, drove his bayonet into Bo's chest.

Time collapsed.

I felt myself separate from my body as though I had become air, floating above the scene. The rape seemed to last for hours, though it could have been minutes.

When it was over, Mai and I laid there bloody, broken, and covered in dirt. Just a few feet away, Bo lay motionless in a pool of red.

I don't remember the pain. I only remember the burning sun on my face and the sound of the wind in the trees as I crawled to Bo, calling out his name. His hand was sticky with blood when I touched it. His eyes were still open.

The forest was silent.

I looked over at Mai, grasped my necklace and slipped into darkness.

I woke to the feeling of arms around me—Mai, lifting me out of the dirt, struggling to load me onto the cart.

"I need you to lift yourself," she said, voice trembling. I raised my arm weakly, trying to pull myself up as she pushed from behind.

Once I was on the cart, the pain crashed over me, and I wailed, "Bo needs a doctor! The city has the best doctors!"

My voice was hoarse. My limbs trembled. I kept fading in and out.

But Mai already knew what I couldn't yet accept—Bo was gone.

She had placed his body next to me on the cart. I reached for his hand, still warm, and rubbed my thumb across his palm like I used to when we were little.

"It's okay, Bo," I whispered. "We'll get you help."

When we arrived, the entire village came to a standstill.

Then my mother screamed.

It was a sound I had never heard before—raw, gut wrenching, from a place beyond language. Her voice cut through the stillness as she ran to the cart. She carried Bo's lifeless body in her arms, her cries echoing through the village.

"My boy!" she cried. "My son—how could this have happened?"

Mai's father rushed to Mai's side and took her into his home. He cleaned the blood from her face and the cuts on her arms with water warmed over the fire. He wrapped her feet in strips of cotton and gave her rice porridge, which she could barely swallow. He never asked questions, never pried—just sat nearby with a hand resting gently on her shoulder when the sobs overtook her.

Khang did the same for me. He held me upright, gently dabbing at my bruises with a damp cloth, his touch careful and steady. My arms ached and my legs trembled, but Khang kept cleaning. He whispered prayers into my hair—words I barely understood, but felt. He didn't try to question me or make sense of what had happened. He just stayed by my side trying to comfort me until I fell asleep.

When I shook from the cold and woke in night, Khang was there and wrapped his jacket around me until I drifted back asleep.

The next two days were the hardest.

Bo's body had been wrapped in a cotton cloth and placed in a pine box, stored in the shed outside. I couldn't bear the thought of him out there in the dark, alone in the cold. It felt wrong, like I was abandoning him. But Mother insisted he was already with the ancestors. She told us to light a candle at the altar, and that his spirit is at rest.

Bo would be buried under the tree next to my father. Incense drifted into the sky, but I couldn't smell them. I could only see my mother sitting motionless beside the fresh dirt, her hands clenched in her lap.

My bruises healed faster than my heart. It took two weeks before the swelling in my face receded, before the wounds began to scab. I refused to eat. I was thinning out, shrinking, disappearing from the inside out.

I couldn't speak Bo's name without trembling. I kept seeing his face—his last breath, his eyes wide in disbelief.

When we were children, I used to tell Bo stories to help him fall asleep. He was scared of the dark, of thunder, of being alone. I made up tales of dragons that roared in the sky to bring rain for the crops. Of earth spirits that played tricks and stole shadows. I once gave him a red pouch with a jasmine petal inside and told him it would make him brave. He wore it every day.

Bo would follow me everywhere, asking questions that made me laugh: "Minh, do ants cry when it rains?" or "Why does the moon follow us home?"

I used to say that he was my shadow.

Now, I had none.

I sat by the creek one afternoon, soaking my feet and staring into the water. I whispered for him. I prayed he was with our father in heaven. That he wasn't afraid.

Mai came quietly and sat on the rocks beside me. Neither of us spoke. She reached out, but I pulled away.

For weeks, I didn't go to the market. Mother and Khang worked the fields alone. I watched from afar as Mai walked the same trail, we had taken that day—the trail that had destroyed everything.

Another day, as I ground herbs outside, Mai approached again.

"You have to move forward, Minh," she said. "You have to live."

I turned away.

"You said to bring him!" I shouted. "If we just left my brother at home, he would be alive!"

Mai's voice cracked, "I didn't...I didn't know—"

She stepped forward, tears rising. "I lost someone, too."

I stared at her.

"Bo...he wasn't just your brother," she whispered. "He was mine, too. I think about him every day. His laughter, his questions. How he tried to carry those heavy jars even when they were too big for him."

Her voice shook. "I blame myself every day Minh. I was just trying to help. I thought he'd enjoy the city. I thought—" she faltered, "I thought it would be good for all of us."

Tears streamed down her cheeks. "But I was wrong. I hear his screams in my sleep. I wake up gasping. You're not the only one who's suffering, Minh."

I looked at her—really looked. Her face was thinner, eyes darker, like mine. We were both wrapped in grief, suffocating beneath it. I wanted to speak, but the words wouldn't come.

Three months later, Mai married Vinh.

Rumors of a child made out of wedlock.

There was no ceremony, only whispered blessings and a red thread wrapped around their wrists. They hosted a small meal, but I did not attend.

I sat alone by Bo's grave that day, knees drawn to my chest, rocking slowly.

I closed my eyes and whispered his name into the earth.

"Bo...I'm so sorry."

The blossoms on the tree above rustled in the breeze. Somewhere deep inside, I imagined he was listening.

But I would never hear his voice again.

And some parts of me would never bloom.

I used to think love was a simple thread—a tie between two hearts. But grief has a way of tangling everything. I loved Bo. I loved Mai. And now those loves hurt in ways I could never have imagined. The pain sits behind my ribs, in my marrow, in my breath. I carry it like a stone tucked inside my chest, invisible, but too heavy to forget.

CHAPTER 12

PRICE OF RESISTANCE

After Bo's death, my home no longer felt like home. It was a roof, a floor, a cooking fire, and a mother who had aged too quickly from sorrow. Mama's hair had turned to threads of white, and her back bent more each day beneath the weight of what she had lost.

The mornings remained the same: wake before the sun, boil water, pack rice, and step barefoot into the cool paddies. But inside our walls, everything had changed. Grief sat with us at every meal. Silence grew thicker than the soup we shared.

And I knew hatred was growing inside my brother's heart, and it didn't help that other villagers were filling his head with thoughts of revenge.

Khang argued with my mother for weeks. He wanted to join the resistance—Ho Chi Minh's fighters hidden in the jungles, striking from the shadows. Guerrilla fighters who knew the terrain like their own breath, who carried rusted rifles and dreams of liberation. They spoke of freedom, but each man who joined risked not just his life, but his entire families. The Japanese occupation may have seemed like an uneasy alliance on the surface, but the truth underneath was different.

There were beatings in broad daylight, rice stolen from harvest baskets, young girls dragged from their homes in the night. Mothers wailing as their sons were dragged to prison over trumped-up charges—suspicions of sabotage, of harboring weapons, of simply speaking out. Men disappeared without a trace. Some were found in the forest days later, their bodies desecrated. Others were never found at all.

"I will not let you go," Mother whispered one night, clutching Khang's arm. "I cannot bear to lose another son."

But he was already gone in spirit. His fists clenched when Japanese soldiers passed through the village on horseback, their uniforms crisp, boots clean from stolen labor. Khang's eyes followed them with quiet fury.

Then one night, he disappeared.

In the morning, Mother found the note in his room. It read, "I will restore honor to our house. I have joined Ho Chi Minh's army to take back our country."

I understood Khang. He felt as I did—that Bo's death was our failure. He had always been the protector, Father's eldest son. In his mind, he should have stood between us and danger.

Each night after he vanished, I heard Mother crying through the thin wall between our rooms. I could not bring myself to cross the room to comfort her. I was too afraid, too broken. My mind spiraled with images—Khang bitten by a snake, captured, shot in the back, or starving in the jungle.

Water crept into my eyes. I could no longer hold it in.

"I wish you didn't go," I sobbed into the darkness. "I wish you would have stayed."

I needed Khang. He made me feel safe when he was near.

Mother and I avoided speaking of him. But it was hard because even Hooch would come around whining outside our doorstep looking for Khang. I'd throw out scraps and tell him, "I don't know where he went but he isn't here." Hooch would eat the scraps then slowly leave.

Things seemed to be improving, I didn't hear Mother crying as often, until one day, at the market, we saw a little boy kick a ball into the street. He nearly got run over by a car. Mother gasped and collapsed to the dirt, clutching her belly.

"No, no, no!" she cried. "I don't want to lose him, too."

I wrapped my arms around her.

"It will be okay," I whispered. "Everything will be alright now."

When we left the market that day and returned home, we prayed and hoped for Khang's return. We even made offerings to the ancestors begging them to watch over him.

Then we returned to what we knew—cultivating the land, drawing strength from routine. I checked in on Mai's parents now and then, asking where Mai and Vinh had moved. They said Vinh had taken his business to the city—Hanoi. Mai was pregnant now, they said. They were doing well.

I began to wonder—was that why Mai rushed the wedding? Maybe she was pregnant from that horrific day. Maybe she had no time to grieve like I had. I began to soften toward her. Though I once blamed her for insisting Bo come with us that day, we had both suffered at the hands of those men. Her life had simply taken a different path.

Then, a man came into my life.

His name was Quang.

At first, I wanted nothing to do with him. My heart was still tangled in grief and fear, and I had no interest in soft words or borrowed promises. When he spoke to me, I listened politely but only nodded. I rarely answered with more than a sentence. Some days, I even hoped he would take the hint and stop coming around.

But he didn't.

His presence was quiet, but constant. There was something steady in him. Not the kind of man who dazzled or demanded attention, but the kind who waited patiently, who didn't need to be noticed to be present.

He started visiting the market on days I helped Mother sell rice. I told myself he wasn't interested in me. Outside of small conversations about grain or price, we rarely spoke. But Mother insisted I give him a chance.

I began watching him, always busy with work, hauling his own sacks of grain, loading and unloading carts by himself. There was a humble dignity in his labor, something honest in the way he moved with purpose.

Eventually, his steadiness wore down the edges of my suspicion. One afternoon, when he offered to walk me home, I didn't say no. We talked about the weather at first, then about the rice fields, then about his parents—both gone before he turned twenty. He lived alone on the farm he'd inherited, a few miles away.

He had no siblings, never dated, and no expectations of me. Just quiet soft eyes, a kind heart, and dry and cracked hands like my father's, like mine.

He never tried to impress me. That, more than anything, I liked about him.

When I spoke, I noticed my words didn't scare him away. He never interrupted me. Never judged. He listened. Really listened.

When I told him I missed my brother, he didn't try to fix the silence that followed. He let it be. When I cried, he comforted me.

When I felt sick, he would bring me boiled ginger tea and asked if I'd eaten anything.

The first time Quang reached for my hand; his touch was so gentle I barely noticed. I only felt the warmth of his palm. It had been a long time since I'd let someone touch me without flinching. But in that moment with him, I felt safe.

We fell in love slowly, over harvests and hushed talks beneath the tamarind tree. He never asked for more than I was ready to give, and when he rubbed his thumb across my cheek, I felt truly seen.

It took nearly two years before I let myself call him my suitor. And even then, it felt like saying goodbye to the fear I had worn like armor.

We eloped with a simple handfasting ceremony—just Mother, Uncle Po, Aunt Tam, Nguyet, and a few of Quang's kin. A red cord bound our hands as incense curled into the warm air. I wore a yellow *áo dài* that Aunt Tam had dyed with turmeric and stitched by hand. There was no feast, only boiled peanuts and rice cakes, but I remember thinking I had never tasted anything so good.

That night, I left my mother's home to live with Quang. I arrived at his house with petals still in my hair and dreams clinging to me like dew.

He stood in the doorway, holding a small oil lamp, its flame flickering in the breeze.

"I will wait," he whispered in the candlelight, touching my chin gently, "as long as you want."

And for the first time in a long while, I wasn't afraid of what came next.

The room was silent, except for the night's insects outside and the steady pulse of both our hearts.

The wedding had ended only a few moments ago. Our cheeks still warm and flush from rice wine.

I undid my dress, slipping it slowly off my body, down until it touched the floor.

I reached out and took Quang's hand pressing it against my soft tender breasts, and whispered, "I am ready."

He took his other hand placing it firmly behind my head, grasping my hair, we leaned in, foreheads almost touching.

His warm embrace, his soft wet lips pressing against mine, I lost all control.

Just as we laid on the bed and he was about to insert himself in me we heard three big bangs at the door.

BANG! BANG! BANG!

I shrieked and pulled the bedsheet up over my chest. Quang stood up, rushing toward the door, grabbing a curved stick from beside the mat.

A voice called out, hoarse, desperate, and panicked, "Minh! It's me! Open quickly!"

Quang unlatched the door, and a young man—muddy, barefoot, face soaked in sweat—fell into the room.

It was Tuan, who lived near my cousin Nguyet, who I hadn't seen since we were children.

"What is it?" I asked, my voice rising.

"It's your brother, Khang," he said between gasps. "He's back. They shot him—the Japanese shot him. He's at your mother's house.

"No," I whispered. As I drifted off feeling faint, like the world was tilting around me.

"Please, come. Hurry."

Tuan's words, "Hurry" snapped me back into my body.

Without a word, Quang grabbed his tunic. I clutched my wedding robe tightly around me, running barefoot across the wooden floor, tying my sash as I went.

We ran, barefoot through the dark, rice wine still on our breath, candlelight still on our skin.

Quang and I arrived at Mother's home, breathless and soaked in the night's dew.

Inside Mother's hut, my brother Khang lay on a straw mat, his tunic torn open. His chest heaved, rising and falling in shallow gasps. Blood soaked through a rag bandage pressed against his ribs. His eyes fluttered half-closed. My mother knelt beside him, tears streaking her wrinkled cheeks.

"Khang! It's me!"

He coughed, his voice brittle.

"Khang!" I dropped to my knees. "Hold on!"

"It's good to see you, sis," he wheezed.

"Don't worry we are going to take you to the hospital."

Gunfire echoed in the distance. Flashlights flickered in the trees. Japanese patrols combed the area.

"We can't stay," Quang said. "If they find him—"

"I'll run," Khang coughed. He tried to stand, collapsing in pain.

Mother pleaded, "We can't move him!"

I racked my mind. Thinking of the wound, the deep gash in Khang's side, and suddenly remembered...

"The butcher!" I gasped. "He knows how to treat wounds. He owns livestock and I've seen him stitch pigs and goats before!"

"Will he help?" Quang asked.

"Of course, he will."

"We have to lift him," Quang said.

Khang was like dead weight, he couldn't stand on his own.

Tuan and my husband lifted him one arm around each of their shoulders. They carried him outside, under the cover of darkness as we made our way down the path to Mai's.

The butcher was boiling bones outside, his wife beside him. When they saw us, they acted fast.

"Inside, before anyone sees."

The butcher swept his table clear. Khang was laid on his back. The butcher peeled back the soaked rags.

"Bullet grazed the lung," he muttered. "Deep, but clean. He's lucky."

Uncle Hung couldn't find an exit wound.

"I'm going to have to extract the bullet," he said.

Searching around in his tool box, he pulled out his metal forceps, sterilizing them over an open flame. He looked at Khang and said, "This is going to hurt, please remain as still as you can."

He looked up at all of us in the room and said, "Hold him down." We did.

As the forceps went into Khang's stomach he screamed loud, then passed out. He pulled the bullet from my brother's body with ease, and dropped it into a basin. Blood kept pouring out. The butcher didn't flinch, he poured rice wine over the wound, then threaded a curved needle, and sewed the wound shut with thread meant for livestock.

We held our breath through every stitch.

By dawn, the bleeding slowed.

Khang would live.

The rooster crowed as pale light broke over the paddies.

I sat on a wooden stool just outside the butcher's hut, wedding robe stained with blood and soil. My hands still trembling in my lap.

Throughout the night I changed my brother's bandages when they became soaked with his blood. I prayed time and time again, until the bleeding ceased.

Inside, Khang lay motionless, wrapped tightly in layers of clean linen. Quang tended the fire. Mother hummed lullabies under her breath. Lianne knelt beside Khang, fanning his fevered face.

Overlooking the horizon, I dreamed of beginning a new life today—of being a wife, starting a family.

War had crept into our wedding bed. It had stolen our first night. Stolen joy. But not hope.

Quang came to sit beside me.

"You should rest," he said gently.

I shook my head, "Not until he is awake."

We sat in silence for a while.

"I imagined our first morning as husband and wife would be different," I said, offering a small, tired smile.

Quang took my hand.

"We'll have our time," he said. "When peace finds us again."

I leaned my head on his shoulder. Despite everything, I felt grateful—for Quang's calm strength, for the butcher's kindness, and most of all, that my brother was still breathing.

In the days that followed, Khang's breathing steadied. The fever finally broke. The butcher spooned goat broth into his mouth and pressed cool cloths to his forehead. Mother never left his side. I helped Mai's mother prepare soups and swept the floor in quiet gratitude.

One afternoon, Khang finally opened his eyes. His voice was weak but clear.

He told us how he'd been shot.

"There was a group of prisoners," he said slowly. "Civilians. They were being marched into the forest. No trials. Just...execution."

His jaw tightened. "Our unit ambushed the Japanese guards. We got a few of them out. But then reinforcements came. We had to scatter. I was hit while covering the retreat."

His eyes darkened. "I was separated. Disoriented. I thought I wouldn't make it back."

He paused. Swallowed.

"Until Hooch found me."

He smiled faintly, but there was pain behind it.

"That old dog helped me get my bearings. Stayed right by me. I thought I wasn't far from home, but I didn't know which way to go. Then a Japanese soldier came out of the trees. He had a rifle. He was going to finish me off..."

Khang's voice broke.

"But Hooch," he said. "He jumped at the soldier. Bit his arm—hard enough to make him drop the gun. That gave me just enough time to run."

He looked away.

"He saved me. Loyal until the end. I escaped and heard a shot ring out; it must have been at Hooch."

I felt my throat tighten. Hooch had been with us for years—our protector. Losing him cut deep. But to lose my brother would have shattered us.

"I thought I was going to die," Khang whispered. "All I could think was...I wanted to see Ma again."

Mother took his hand and pressed it to her cheek. "You came back," she whispered. "That's all that matters."

That day Khang vowed never to return to his unit. He decided, he would recover and return to helping Mother tend the fields.

One week later, Khang could sit up, and began walking around the village again.

Quang and I returned home. The red lanterns from our wedding sagged with age. The feast had spoiled. But the air inside was still ours.

That night, finally, we were alone. No interruptions. No knocking. No gunfire.

Just us.

I lit a candle and stood by the mat.

This time, when we laid beside each other, there was only quiet.

Only two hearts finding each other in the candlelight.

We finally consummated our marriage.

CHAPTER 13

MY BROTHER'S BATTLE

During my brother's recovery, the village buzzed with tension. Japanese patrols grew more aggressive. Young men whispered of resistance; elders told them to be quiet. One wrong word, one careless glance could cost us our lives.

I would frequent Mother's home to check on Khang, bringing herbs and boiled soup to speed his healing.

In truth, Khang rarely spoke of what he saw in the jungle, but his silence said more than words ever could.

Still word spread quickly. By the end of the week, villagers whispered of a daring rescue. Whispers grew into stories—how his unit had ambushed a Japanese convoy, how they freed political prisoners destined for secret execution sites in the forest. Some villagers called him a brave hero. Others, reckless.

He said nothing to defend either view.

One night, while we shelled peanuts under a sky dense with stars, he finally spoke.

"They lined them up," he murmured, eyes fixed on the fire. "Villagers. Suspected rebels. No trials, just accusations. One by one, they marched them into the jungle. Shots would ring out. Then silence."

I could hardly breathe.

Khang's voice dropped lower. "There were women...bruised thighs. Men with split lips and broken teeth. Children who wouldn't speak, marched together in chains. They say Japan is our ally. But allies don't steal your food, burn your fields, or take your daughters in the night."

I felt sick. I had heard the rumors. But now it was my brother saying them aloud.

He told me of how the Japanese confiscated rice stores meant for villages and shipped them north to feed their troops. Of how, in some provinces, entire hamlets had been emptied—young men conscripted into forced labor, young women taken "for comfort."

"There was a girl younger than you," he said. "Tied up in the back of a truck. Her dress ripped; hair shaved off. She looked at me like she already accepted that fact that she would die."

Tears welled in my eyes, but I didn't let them fall. I took my brother's hand. It was rough and calloused, like Quang's. Like Father's. But there was a tremble in it now, I had never seen before.

Although my brother carried a scar from his wound the mental scars were worse. From that night on, I noticed his jaw was never fully at rest.

Over time, however, he came back to us. He didn't surrender and give up like my father. He just grew into a stronger version of himself.

He helped mother greatly during that time, clearing the fields, selling in the market, and fixing up the house that was in decay since dads passing.

Although the mood in the village shifted, Khang didn't let the war sway him to leave again.

Japanese soldiers increased their visits to the market, rifles slung across their backs, eyes sweeping every stall. They seized baskets of grain, slapped vendors who asked for payment. Once, a man spoke up when a soldier dragged his sister by the arm. They beat him until he could no longer walk. No one intervened.

Then one evening when the market was quiet and Khang and I were making rice sales; a man appeared with a bandage on his arm. I instantly froze. Could I get a pound of rice please, said the solider. I fumbled and dropped my bag, Khang stepped right in, and said I have one right here. He didn't stutter until he looked up and met the man's eyes.

In front of Khang stood the very same Japanese soldier that Hooch sunk his teeth into.

Khang's body tensed, his breath catching in his throat. He recognized the soldier instantly—he was the one who had nearly shot him before Hooch intervened. Khang's heart pounded so loudly, I could almost hear it.

But then the soldier did something unexpected.

He nodded, and said "Thank You!" glancing down at the bag of rice.

Khang didn't speak. He couldn't. His hands remained locked in place, as if even the smallest movement might trigger recognition.

But the soldier said nothing else. He took the bag, gave a shallow bow, and walked off.

Khang's shoulders sagged as he exhaled slowly.

I watched as the soldier disappeared into the crowd.

"That was him, the one from the forest. The one Hooch bit."

Khang nodded, eyes still fixed on the horizon. "I thought he was going to finish what he started."

I placed a hand on his arm. "He didn't."

Khang looked down, finally breaking the stillness. "Maybe he didn't recognize me."

"Or maybe he did," I said. "And he felt guilty."

We stood there in silence, the air between us thick with everything unspoken.

At night, patrols came stomping through the fields. Searching for hidden radios. Maps. Men.

Soft spoken undertones grew louder. Resistance in the North was building. Guerillas cut supply and telegraph lines, derailed trains, and poisoned wells used by enemy soldiers. The Viet Minh, led by Ho Chi Minh, struck swiftly, vanishing into hills before retribution could follow.

One evening, Quang and I passed a burned-out hut near the river. Blackened beams, ashes blowing into the water like dry leaves. A family had lived there. Now no one spoke their name aloud.

"They had a daughter," I said softly. "I think about ten, her father accused as a rebel so they burned their house to the ground."

Still, young men slipped away at night—drawn to the jungle like moths to flame. Some returned with bullet wounds or hollow eyes. Others didn't return at all.

I visited Mai's parents one morning and found their neighbor's son, seventeen, vanished one night. Gone. "Said he couldn't bear to see one more girl taken. Said he'd rather die with a gun in his hand."

That same day, Khang and I would visit our father and brother's graves.

Standing over the graves and looking down upon the stones we had laid there, Khang asked, "You think they'd be proud of me?"

I didn't answer because I didn't know.

I only knew I was proud.

Deep in the jungle, others like Khang fought, bled, and died—

so that maybe, one day, Vietnam would belong to her own people again, and that to me was something to be proud of.

When we returned home to Mother's, a letter waited tucked in the doorframe. Folded rice paper. Neat handwriting. Sealed in red wax.

I held it in my hand, heart pounding.

A new chapter was about to begin.

CHAPTER 14

LETTERS FROM THE CITY

Dear Minh,

I hope this letter finds you healthy and well. Vinh and I are living in Hanoi now; can you believe it? The streets are lined with lanterns and flowers, and everything smells of coffee and silk. He is working with merchants who make truck deliveries from Hai Phong (another city in northern Vietnam). I sew at a shop that sells Japanese dresses. I think of you often. You should visit. There is so much life here.

Love,
Mai

I would write back:

Dear Mai,

I am married, I hope you and Vinh are well. I have so much to tell you. My brother is safe and home. I would en-joy coming to the city for a visit.

Minh

We exchange letters every few weeks. I looked forward to putting our past behind us. I still felt the pain of losing Bo, but I also felt the pain of losing Mai.

In her letters, Mai told me about their apartment above the market, the way the rain sounded on the tile roof, the smells of roasted peanuts and jasmine tea wafting in through the open shutters. She had a baby—a girl. Her name was Anh, peaceful. I sent a bundle of swaddling cloth and herbs for the baby's colic.

Through our exchanges, I discovered Mai already had a second baby on the way.

She wrote again:

Minh,

I'm pregnant, again. Can you believe it? A second child. I can feel him moving inside already. This time I think it's a boy. Vinh says he wants to name him after the dragon—the creature of strength and blessing. I don't mind as long as the baby is healthy. The midwife says I will deliver come summer. I dream sometimes—of our children playing together.

Love,

Mai

After a year, of trying—Quang and I still couldn't bear children. We prayed to the ancestral shrines, boiled herbs, and counted many moons.

But my womb stayed quiet.

I began to dream of Bo's face, over and over—that last terrible moment, of me reaching my hand out to grab his.

I woke in the night drenched in sweat, with a scream caught in my throat.

I told no one but wanted to tell Mai.

Another letter came

Dear Minh,

We named our baby Hein. He is handsome, Minh. I hope you meet him some day. He is handsome like his father, and is already forming words. I've sent you a small gift—some cloth, and a fertility tonic that an old woman swears by. Maybe it will help. I pray for you always.

Mai

I shared with Mai that I was having fertility issues, but she simply pushed too hard. Mai would send herbs and teas to promote healing and charms symbolizing fertility and youth.

It began to bother me that Mai left me behind to move to the big city. All her dreams as a child had come true, living with her wealthy husband in a beautiful home in the city.

Although mine had, too, the one thing I wanted the most was children. Mai never wanted kids, she always planned on traveling.

Another letter arrived.

A photo. And drawings her children made.

I could not finish reading.

Tears welled up in my eyes as I began to wonder what was wrong with me. *Am I infertile? Was I being punished, why couldn't I get pregnant?*

I was so bitter at Mai, she was the queen of fertility, and I couldn't even experience pregnancy with my husband Quang.

I didn't reply.

I folded her letters into the same wooden box where I placed my locket, the one we had picked out at the market after our bike ride. I had almost thrown it away after Bo's death but something made me keep it. Maybe it was because our friendship never died, only took a brief pause.

Weeks later, and no letter arrived, but someone in a fancy car arrived in the village. When they stepped out of the car, I could barely recognize them in their white suits, western hats, and summer dresses.

It was Mai holding two children in each arm with a third in her belly. Behind her stood Vinh, still handsome as ever, giving his typical grin.

My husband and I were still dirty from working the fields earlier that day.

Mai waved. "How are you?" she shouted.

"I'm good, I'm really well," I replied.

Mai put her hand on mine, "We need to catch-up, tell me everything."

Vinh and my husband decided to watch the kids while Mai and I took a walk down along the river.

As we walked, I told Mai about my brother, how he was shot, how her father saved him, on my wedding night with Quang. I talked about the farm, the land we cultivated together. And even that Khang is starting to meet girls in the market.

Mai told me about the city; how extravagant it was and how her husband is a wealthy businessman. She dragged on and on about how great things were.

Suddenly, I started to feel like my life was stationary.

Mai said I should visit a doctor with her in the city, and maybe they could recommend new fertility herbs.

She said she came to move her father and mother to Hanoi and bought them a small meat store in front in the market. That

Lianne, her mother, would still be able to boil and serve soup just to a lot more people than in our little village.

Mai asked me to consider moving there with her, that her husband Vinh could hire my husband to work as a truck driver alongside him.

I felt like Mai had forgotten where she came from and was beginning to look down on me and Quang's life. The city had changed her.

She was no longer Mai, the inseparable friend I grew up with.

She traded her village home for brick and mortar, no longer labored long hours with me in the sun, and was even learning a new language.

Mai said, "I know you don't mind being dirty, and working hard in the fields, but you've outgrown this, I want you to be by my side." She kept up, "You know you break your back day in and day out, and for what, to just get by. It's not a good environment to have a child."

Mai reached out her arms, placing them on my shoulders. "In the city the doctors can find out why you can't bear children and fix it."

I grabbed Mai's arms and pushed them away from me.

"My life is just fine, thank you. Our parents had us in the village and we grew up just fine. And you want to know what is wrong with me, it is that I was raped, and you were too."

Mai's smile turned to a frown.

"I still have nightmares of my brother; don't you get that? You might have moved on Mai, but I didn't. Did you ever question, question if your first child is even Vinh's?"

Mai stood there, frozen in shock, a single tear rolled down her cheek. I immediately regretted my words, I never wanted to say what I said, but there it was, out in the open for all to see. I tried to speak but nothing came out.

The next second, I felt a sharp sting across the left side of my cheek. Mai slapped me.

I looked up trying to focus my eyes and there was Vinh standing just a few feet behind Mai with her two children.

Mai's children wanted to meet their mother's friend, so they decided to follow us down by the stream.

Mai shouted, "I was already pregnant before that incident, me and Vinh made love at the market the day..." Mai paused, angry and hurt, "forget it."

She backed away from me, "I was your only friend."

She turned and hugged her husband, "I'm so sorry Vinh, I promise you she is yours."

Mai never told Vinh about the rape. She tried to conceal it from him. But the whole village had known, and I am sure word reached the city about it.

Vinh held Mai tight in his arms. "I know Mai, I've known the whole time."

He took Mai's hand and said, "Let's go."

I stood frozen, watching as my best friend walked away from me. She returned to her car without looking back. Vinh buckled the children into their seats, climbed in beside her, and together they drove away.

My face crumpled like rice paper in the rain, I cried, "Oh no... what have I done?"

My legs felt like they no longer belonged to me. I stumbled up the stairs, tripping as I reached for the door.

Quang stepped outside; concern written across his face. "What happened? Is everything alright?"

I couldn't answer. I steadied myself against him, then collapsed into his arms, sobbing into his shirt.

The next morning, I went to Mai's parents' home, hoping to speak with her. But when I arrived, the car was gone, and the house was silent. Her parents were nowhere to be seen. I rushed to my mother's house. Mother told me solemnly, "They packed up and left last night."

Panic gripped my chest. I ran home, sat at the table, and poured my heart into another letter. I mailed it immediately. I had to apologize. I had to believe there was still a chance Mai could forgive me.

Months passed, but no reply ever came.

I had wounded Mai deeply. I knew it. And I knew I had to do whatever it took to mend what I had broken. Quang and I began planning a trip to the city. I was determined to find her—to look her in the eye and make things right. But before the plans could be finalized, I discovered I was pregnant.

The argument with Mai had happened just before I conceived.

As much as I longed to see her, I couldn't bring myself to risk the journey. I chose to wait until after the baby was born, in the fall.

Despite everything, I felt a flicker of hope. I was going to be a mother.

Carrying life inside me felt like holding a fragile flame in a world full of wind. Every morning, I woke early, placing both hands over my belly, whispering promises to the tiny soul growing within me. I had waited so long for this—to feel life stirring beneath my ribs, to dream of small hands grasping my fingers. Years of prayers, of quiet disappointment, of hiding tears when other women in the village announced their pregnancies. Now, at last, my body had opened like spring soil, ready to grow something beautiful.

Quang was overjoyed, but cautious. "Don't overwork," he said constantly. "Rest more. Eat more." He treated me as if I were glass. But inside, I felt stronger than I had in years.

The early months weren't easy. I was sick every morning, dizzy by noon, and exhausted by dusk. My emotions swung like a bell—joy, fear, anger, wonder, sorrow. One moment I'd be singing as I folded baby linens; the next I'd be crying over a cracked bowl.

Sometimes I'd sit by the window and wonder: Would it be a boy with Quang's quiet eyes? Or a girl with my stubborn chin? I imagined teaching her to braid her hair, or holding my son's hand as we walked to the market. I imagined laughter, little sandals by the door, the scent of rice and steamed greens in the evening as I fed a hungry child.

The nights were the hardest. The silence of the countryside would be broken by distant gunfire or rumors from neighbors—skirmishes nearby, soldiers moving through villages, boys disappearing into the jungle. I would lie awake with one hand on my belly, whispering prayers: "Please let this child live. Please let this world be kind."

I wrote letters I never sent—to Mai, and sometimes to my future child. In those pages, I poured out my regrets and hopes. "I am afraid," I wrote one night, "but I will not be defeated by fear. You deserve a brave mother."

By the sixth month, my body was fully transformed. My back ached, and my ankles swelled. But I walked the fields slowly, letting the sun warm my face. The village women gave me sweet rice wrapped in banana leaves, muttering folk blessings under their breath. An old neighbor tied a red thread around my wrist for luck. My mother gave me a handwoven blanket she had saved since I was born.

"Whether boy or girl," she said, "this child is already loved."

Quang built a tiny wooden cradle. I caught him once with his hand resting on my belly as he whispered a name, Lan, for a girl, or Cuu for a boy.

In my final month, I was so large I could barely bend over. Quang laughed gently as he slipped my sandals on for me. "The baby will have your stubbornness," he joked. I wanted to believe that. I wanted my child to inherit my strength, my fire—but also Quang's patience, his quiet kindness.

One day, while washing clothes by the river, I felt a sharp pain ripple through me. I clutched my stomach and gasped. The other women rushed over, helping me home. The baby wasn't ready yet—but the signs had begun. The wait was almost over.

Then came the night. The air was thick with fog, it was unbelievably hot, and you could see heat lighting in the distance with no thunder. My water broke just after midnight. Quang had already brought the midwife.

Pain came in waves, fierce and wild. My mother held my hand, her voice familiar and calming. The midwife prepared the towels. Sweat poured down my face. I screamed once, then bit down hard. But I would not surrender. I was bringing life into this world, and I would see it through.

At dawn, the cries of a newborn filled the room. I was shaking, exhausted, soaked with sweat and tears—but when they placed her in my arms, I wept from a place deeper than I knew existed.

A daughter. A perfect, tiny daughter.

She had a full head of black hair and a serious expression, as if she already knew the world she was entering. I named her Lan—orchid—because she had bloomed in the darkest season.

I kissed her brow and whispered, "You were worth every tear. I will be strong for you. I will love you beyond all measure."

CHAPTER 15

INDEPENDENCE WAS IN OUR GRASP

That autumn, the world changed. In September of 1945, Japan surrendered unconditionally to the Allied Forces—France, Great Britain, the United States, Russia, and China. Japanese troops began retreating from Vietnam, and Ho Chi Minh, the rebel leader under whom my brother had fought, declared our nation's independence.

The summer of 1945 carried with it a wind of change so strong, it swept through even the smallest rice-farming villages like ours. We felt it in the way people stood taller, in the laughter that returned to the markets, and in the stories that came drifting in from travelers and Viet Minh soldiers who emerged from the jungle no longer hiding, but walking proudly through city streets lined with flags and children playing barefoot.

The Japanese had retreated, their empire fractured, after five years of occupying Vietnam. On September 2nd, in the great square of Hanoi, our leader Ho Chi Minh stood before thousands and declared what we had only dared to whisper—Vietnam was free.

His voice, broadcast over the crackling speakers, reached even our village through the battery radio set placed near the village well. We gathered—men, women, children, the elderly—with eyes shining as he read our Declaration of Independence. "All men are created equal. The Creator has given us certain inviolable rights: the right to life, the right to be free, and the right to achieve happiness."

I remember standing shoulder-to-shoulder with Mama and Quang. Some cried. Old men leaned on their canes and nodded, speaking softly to each other about the French, then the Japanese, and the dream they'd almost given up on. Women clutched their babies close and whispered prayers of thanks. Even the children, unaware of the full weight of history, sensed something sacred was happening. They danced with the Viet Minh soldiers who laughed, lifted them high, and played games in the city streets that had once echoed with gunfire.

After decades of imperial rule, we finally dared to hope.

It was a good year. Crops flourished. The rains were gentle. The harvest overflowed. My husband Quang and I worked side-by-side, our hands never idle, our smiles more frequent than frowns. Our daughter, Lan, took her first steps beneath the sky full of peace.

Even in our village, excitement swelled. The abandoned French posts and prisons were being destroyed. Any French business was swiftly moved into. People, mended old fences, shared more freely, and planted more diligently that year.

But not all things had healed.

Father's old ox died unexpectedly, collapsing under the summer sun. With no money for a new one, Mother's fields sat unplowed. We considered selling a section of our own crop to help, but before the week ended, Uncle Po arrived at her door.

Uncle Po came in clean clothes, he looked clean cut, and

carried with him a new energy. He brought with him not one, but two strong young oxen—one white, one brown—and handed their reins to my mother with a grin. "You'll be fine now," he said. "These ones will outlast your old ox."

We laughed, even Mother.

Nguyet played with my little daughter, and we laughed and shared stories throughout the day.

But Po's visit wasn't just to deliver livestock. He came with news. He was moving to the city.

The French had built a railroad during the occupation, then abandoned it as their empire crumbled. Now it sat, rusting in the heat, but with potential. Po saw it. He had saved enough from selling rubber, and now he could afford to hire a staff of men to tap the rubber trees, mix the acid, and carry the hardened sheets to his shop in the city. With the train line open, he could skip the French and Japanese trucks and send his goods straight to other cities—directly from producer to consumer.

"It's time," he said to us all. "There is peace. The future is in the city."

Before he left, Po gifted us a new cart—strong, with wheels that didn't squeak or seize. He said it was time our family had one that rolled smoothly over muddy roads.

We watched him go, Aunt Tam and Nguyet riding alongside him in the cart as they left for the newly freed city square where he would soon buy one of the largest and most elegant houses in all of Hue.

Uncle Po flourished during that time. He kept his rubber trees, but no longer needed to wake before dawn to check the buckets or wait days for enough sap. He smiled more. His home, a French villa, a beautiful and upscale home built from yellow painted stone, its charm accentuated by elegant white shutters, tall pillars, carved bannisters, and grand archway over the door. Though not as large or lavish as some of the city's grandest villas, those boasting in-ground pools and sprawling pavilions, it still carried the dignified grace of French colonial architecture, with its long corridors, open balconies, and symmetrical design. Nestled within a lush and carefully maintained garden and flowering vines, the villa seamlessly blended elements of a traditional Hue-garden house, creating an atmosphere of refined serenity. Inside, tall ceilings and tiled floors with French chandeliers hung from wooden rafters, lotus-patterned carvings adorned the doorframes, and lacquered Vietnamese cabinets. A central courtyard allowed natural light to pour in, and small stone pathways meandered through flowering trees and potted orchids.

My husband and I would visit his new home when we carried rice to the market to sell. We were mesmerized by the sheer size and beauty. Often, Mother would tag along. While my husband and I sold rice, Mother tended to our baby at her brother's store. She once said, "I have never seen so much wealth in one place." Uncle Po and his wife were always going over lists, sealing crates, directing men as they loaded rubber onto freight trains that traveled across a free Vietnam. It was a world so far from our muddy paddies that it felt like another country altogether.

Nguyet, my cousin, was growing up so fast. She loved when I came to visit. She doted on my baby girl Lin, dressing her in tiny clothes, pretending to put makeup on her with crushed berries and chalk. She always had crayons and let my daughter color the walls of their courtyard.

During those visits, a new bond formed—one that helped fill the space Mai had left behind when she stopped writing. I still regretted the horrible words I said that day, and when my baby was old enough to be without breast feeding, I promised myself to run to Mai and beg forgiveness.

In the meantime, Nguyet became my companion, my comfort, my reminder that love could grow again, even in the shadow of regret.

That year sped by so quickly.

We believed in new beginnings.

For our country. For our family. For ourselves.

CHAPTER 16

THE CELEBRATION OF HO CHI MINH

December 1946 France invaded again; they wanted to reclaim the territory they lost to the Japanese. But Ho Chi Minh was ready. He enlisted many bright young men to fight. Vietnam for the first time in 100 years tasted freedom, and we weren't going to bow down and give it up lightly.

The First Indo-China war was bloody, and hard-fought. Wounded Viet Minh soldiers would crawl through the jungle to our village for help. The villagers played their part in the war. We hid the wounded, carried them into the city hospitals on our carts for treatment. We donated what supplies and food we could to support the Vietnamese army.

Another two years would pass, the war, no longer on our front lines. The Viet Minh pushed back the French army South of us near Saigon.

But the land was scarred from mortar shells, we saw the men who lost their limbs, and witnessed elders with low morale.

Things were becoming harder, the officers who protected us were seizing 30 percent of what we produced and in return gave us war bonds. A form of currency that you couldn't collect until it was certain our leader was victorious.

News soon came by flyers, a large red sickle and hammer emblem in the corner.

Tattered sheets of paper plastered along the city walls. They bore the image of a thin man with a long beard and eyes that appeared sunk-in into his narrow face. In bold black ink were the words:

"President Ho Chi Minh to speak – Come and witness history."

The news spread like wildfire. As people made arrangements to attend the city hall meeting.

Weeks passed as the event neared.

Then, on the day of Ho Chi Minh's arrival, the rice fields stood empty. The market stalls were half-covered. Children ran ahead of their parents, chattering about how they'd seen the trucks arrive, how the soldiers had marched in carrying red flags slung over their shoulders.

My husband and I followed the crowd of people toward the town square. I had never seen our city so full. Even the oldest men and women came out, hobbling along with sticks and straw hats, whispering to one another about the man who had defied the French, the man who gave us freedom from the Japanese.

He stood on a raised platform surrounded by young Viet Minh soldiers in green uniforms. They stood straight, but not stiff or cruel—they were relaxed, smiling, even playful. One soldier even ruffling a small boy's hair. They seemed...like us.

Then Ho Chi Minh spoke.

His voice wasn't loud, but it filled the space. Steady. Clear. Like a thread pulling every ear and heart toward him.

"We have resisted," he said. "We have suffered long under foreign masters. But we are no longer slaves."

The crowd erupted. I felt myself clapping before I realized my hands were raised.

He continued, "The French say they return to protect us. But who protects us from them? From the taxes, the beatings, the theft of our land?"

People around us shouted, "*Kháng chiến*!"—Resistance! A chant started and rippled outward. Farmers, merchants, students, monks, even barefoot children shouted with fists raised.

Then he paused, eyes scanning the crowd. He spoke slower, like a father to his children.

"We must be united. We must share what we have. Work together, eat together, fight together. No rich, no poor. Only Vietnamese."

Something in that made me pause.

No rich, no poor.

I glanced at my husband. His eyes were wide with awe. But I thought about Uncle Po, who worked so hard to build his business. About the little shop he ran, the men he hired, the profit he earned through sweat and sleepless nights. Would he have to give that up?

But the voice of the crowd drowned my question.

"Unite! Unite!" they shouted.

As Ho Chi Minh stepped down from the platform, he made his way slowly through the sea of people. His hands extended, touching shoulders, blessing children. He passed near us—and for a brief second, he looked directly at me. His hand, weathered and light, reached out and brushed mine.

It felt like touching history.

Quang, gripping my arm, "You touched him, you actually got to touch him!"

There was something childlike in his awe, something pure. In that moment, he believed we were on the right path to a better future.

After the president departed in a black jeep with a single red flag fluttering behind, the crowd began to move again—but this time with direction. Purpose.

Outside the square, officers were sitting with paper sheets spread across their wooden tables, men lined up, signed their name to the pages, enlisting to join the cause. One by one, villagers added their names. My husband gave me a hesitant look; I gripped his arm firmly.

"Not yet," I said. "There will be time."

We walked home, hands clasped, our feet quiet on the road. The sun dipped low, casting long shadows over our house and the new cart Po had gifted us. Our daughter spending the night at Mother's.

My husband and I sat outside in silence for a long time.

"We can win this time," my husband whispered.

"I believe we can," I replied. But something inside me—a small, uncertain part—wondered—at what cost?

CHAPTER 17

THE DAY OF TWO BRIDES

I watched my older brother, Khang, from the edge of the rice paddies. He had always been shy and serious, preferring the rhythm of the river to the chatter of girls. But today, he stood beside a young woman near the market's edge, his eyes lit like lanterns. Her name was Thao. She moved with a quiet grace. Selling bundles of dried herbs and flowers—mint, basil, citronella, jasmine, and tuberose—her stall always blooming with scent and color. Her body was slender but not frail, with light sun-browned skin. Her laugh, light and bright like wind chimes. I had never seen my brother Khang smile that way before.

Khang began walking her home, staying longer at the marketplace, and helping her father fix fishing nets. The war had hardened many, but I saw my brother soften. He even sang again— quiet songs he hadn't hummed since our father died. Love had crept in like the morning fog. The world was changing. War rumbled beyond the fields, but here, in stolen glances and shared tea, a quieter revolution bloomed.

My cousin Nguyet, found someone, too. His name was Long, a rubber shop assistant with calloused hands and a tender voice. His strength wasn't loud or boastful—it was written in the way he carried himself, in the quiet confidence of his movements. He brought her mangoes wrapped in banana leaves and asked about her dreams, not just her chores. I saw the way my friend swept the shop slower now, humming, her cheeks warm with color.

Uncle Po, proud and sentimental, offered to pay for both weddings. "Let them marry on the same day," he declared. "Let joy come in waves."

As we prepared decorations for the wedding and sent out invitations, I thought often of Mai—of her eyes that day when she walked away, the silence that followed, the letter unanswered and gathering dust like a wound that never healed.

My joy for Khang and Nguyet stirred up complicated grief.

One evening, as I sat outside Uncle Po's shop, he came out and sat beside me, lighting his tobacco pipe. He looked at me and gently said, "Minh, something seems to be bothering you."

I hesitated, "I'm just overjoyed that we are a family, I never thought life would be this special." I paused then admitted, "The only thing I am missing is my friend, Mai."

Uncle Po nodded, "Ah yes, I remember how inseparable you two were. Always running through my rubber grove. Your father once told me the two of you could never be apart."

He puffed thoughtfully and added, "Whatever came between you—it can always be fixed. She is your family, too. And family never turns their back on you. Now off to bed," he said, smiling. "We have a wedding to throw tomorrow."

Morning would come, and we would be busy as ever. Making sure Nguyet and Khang's wife fit into their dresses, as Aunt Tam and my mother helped style their hair.

The village gathered under flowered arches built from bamboo. No expense was spared—Uncle Po paid for roasted pig, white lilies, silk dresses, and a golden canopy over the altar. I wore my finest *ao dài* and wept as Khang kissed his bride and Nguyet stepped into the arms of her new husband.

Later the photographer snapped a portrait: everyone standing tall, their faces glowing. But my eyes searched the background, hoping Mai might appear at the edge of the crowd.

She never did.

Still, that day, love reigned. Lanterns floated in the river. Children danced in circles. Drums beat into the night. Laughter echoed between the trees.

For once, the world paused. And in that joy, there was a space for hope.

A small, quiet hope that time and tenderness might one day restore what had been broken.

CHAPTER 18

WHEN THE FIELDS TURNED TO ASH

My daughter was finally walking—little steps on bare feet through the soft dust outside our home. She would toddle after the chickens, arms out, laughing wildly as she played.

Khang had taken a position working on his wife's father's boat. He spent many weeks sailing for fish but quickly rose to first mate. Her father, a man of few words, took to Khang kindly, often sneaking him extra catches to bring home. Khang even helped transport rubber materials for Uncle Po and rice for Quang and I, using those same ships bringing supplies between coastal towns.

Our family was together. Everyone worked harmoniously.

Later, as months passed, Nguyet's belly rounded. I swept beside her at the shop, remembering my own pregnancy. We laughed and shared pickled plum and sour tamarind. When Nguyet gave birth to a boy as handsome as Long, they named him Duy. I held him close and whispered, "You're the hope we prayed for."

Those days lifted my spirit. Yet, as I rocked the baby or swept beside my cousin, my thoughts wandered to Mai. The girl from the creek. The one who had shared my childhood. *If only I could find her again*, I thought. *If only I could say I'm sorry.*

But then the disease came.

It started as yellow tips on the rice stalks, then a sudden browning that spread like wildfire. Bacterial blight and stem rot—the elders recognized it immediately. We tried every method we knew: changing water levels, plucking infected stocks, mixing ash into the soil, even prayer. Nothing worked. The smell of decay hung in the air reminding us that the seasonal grain was ruined.

To save what land we could, we had to burn it. Flames devoured the golden fields my husband and I had worked so hard to cultivate. Mother's fields would rot from the disease, too. For the first time in generations, we would not plant.

We relied on Uncle Po that year, more than ever. He took us in without hesitation.

His home in the city had room for us. His shop sold dried herbs, rice, fabrics, and rubber—whatever villagers needed and could afford. He welcomed us no questions asked. His daughter and I swept floors, dusted shelves, and fed the babies, and we shared quiet afternoons under fans that hummed weakly in the heat.

Nguyet's infant boy was only a few months old. My daughter Lan, now four, played beside him. The children would color with leftover chalk on old receipts. Sometimes Lan liked rocking Duy to sleep. Nguyet and I would sit by the window speaking softly, not about war or crops, but motherhood—about fear, forgiveness, and love.

It was in that stillness that I made the decision.

With no crops to tend, I decided it was time. Lan had grown enough.

I would go find Mai.

I had saved the address she once wrote on the back of an

old letter. It had faded, nearly vanished, but I knew it by heart. I refused to forget it.

"I will go," I told Quang one evening, "to the city. To her."

He nodded. "Go. Find your peace. We'll wait for you."

The next night I packed my bags, and the following morning, I made sure to put on my necklace before heading out the door. My daughter and husband escorted me to the train station.

As I stood in line to purchase a ticket, my eyes swelled, it was the first time I would be leaving my daughter.

On the platform my husband was holding our daughter in his arms. Lan's head tucked against his shoulder, her arms waving at me goodbye.

I smiled through the tears, waved back, and stepped onto the train.

The compartment was crowded, packed with farmers, vendors, and elders with bundles of rice tied to cloth.

As the train pulled away from the station, I felt something shift—not fear, not even hope, but a fierce sense of clarity.

I was going to find her.

I was going to tell her everything.

Even if she didn't forgive me.

Even if she slammed the door.

Even if all I could do was leave the words at her feet.

I had to try.

For us.

For the girls we used to be, and for the women we had become.

CHAPTER 19

THE TRAIN TO FORGIVENESS

The train journey was long and cramped. I was fortunate to find a seat while others would stand holding onto the bars that ran overhead.

I sat beside a soldier asleep on his rifle, a woman was seated behind me with a crying baby, across from me there was an elderly man eating a bag of sunflower seeds, he took a scoop in his hand and reached out placing it into mine. I was thankful, the salty handful of seeds, lasted me the journey. While on the train I decided to people watch, to fain from boredom.

Two students were scribbling in a notebook, others sat with their husbands and children, some read the newspaper. Outside the windows, the land shifted from green farm fields with little wooden huts, to small towns with buildings made of concrete, then to a bustling, unfamiliar city, roaring with steel and vehicles and public buses blanketing the streets.

When I arrived, I was lost. The street names were confusing, and I struggled to find my way. Foreign shop signs were brightly painted. Bicycles zipped past me, horns blaring. I turned the address over and over in my hand, checking to make sure I still held it. Eventually, after several wrong turns and confused directions from impatient shopkeepers, I finally met someone guiding traffic to take the time and show me the street. Once I was on the street, I began walking block by block looking for the address. 107, 120, I had a long way to go since Mai's address was 638 Nguyen Street.

Finally, after walking for what seemed to be hours, I found them.

They didn't see me, but I could see them.

Mai. Vinh. Three children—all hers, I knew it. She had 2 boys, and her girl had grown so much since I last saw her. They walked hand in hand down the sidewalk, Mai's laughter ringing out like wind chimes, pointing into shop windows. Her skin glowed in the sunlight; her smile effortless. I stood frozen, unable to move. My mouth opened, but no sound came.

I couldn't ruin this day. Not now.

I ducked into a small pho restaurant nearby, the smell of broth and herbs wrapping around me like a blanket. I ordered a bowl and picked at it in silence. The hours passed. Evening fell. I sipped on tea, waiting and watching as the sun set behind the city's rooftops. As boredom settled in, I began peeling at the edge of the table's lacquer with my fingernail, tracing faint rings left by old tea cups. I tapped my foot under the table, glanced at the door every few minutes, and folded and unfolded my napkin, trying to pass the time.

Then, with the streets quieter and the sky dimming to purple, and the kids put to sleep, I walked to the door. The door's faded paint was chipped around the edges, and the brass handle felt cool and foreign beneath my fingers. My heart thudded as I reached for it. I hadn't seen Mai in years, not since the falling out that left silence in place of friendship. *What if I wasn't welcome? What if I opened old wounds just by standing here?* I hesitated, my hand hovering, afraid that one knock might unravel whatever peace this home had managed to build without me.

But I couldn't turn back now, not after how far I had come.

I paused, caught my breath, and let the silence settle around me. Then, with a trembling hand, I knocked.

It was Vinh who answered.

He looked older. Tired, but strong. His eyes scanned me for a moment before narrowing slightly.

"Why have you come?" he asked.

"I need to speak to Mai," I said.

His voice was calm but firm. "What makes you think she wants to see you?"

I had no reply. Only tears that welled up in my eyes.

"I think it's best if you leave," Vinh said softly. "Before she sees you."

My lips trembling. "Please, I have to speak to her."

"You've put my wife through enough."

I lowered my head, nodding in agreement, and turned to walk away. But as I stepped off the porch, a thought clung to me, I couldn't give up, but if Vinh is guarding the door—I would try again tomorrow. Maybe, when Vinh was at work. I would wait by the market if I had to. I couldn't let it end like this.

Then from inside I heard her voice.

"Honey, who is it?"

"No one, dear," Vinh replied.

It was now or never.

I turned back, heart pounding, and pushed open the door.

"Mai," I choked inside. "I'm sorry. I'm so sorry."

I collapsed onto the floor, my knees hitting the throw carpet, as I sobbed uncontrollably.

Mai stood in the hallway eyes wide, unsure of how to respond. Her face didn't move at first, her hands gripping a dish towel, her expression unreadable.

But then she knelt.

She reached out and lifted me from the floor.

"Come now," she whispered, wrapping her arms around me. "Come inside."

Mai sat me at her family's kitchen table. She walked over to the sink with a kettle. She put the kettle over the flame and began warming the pot.

"I will make you a tea," she said.

Her kindness, her welcoming nature, how could she be so nice to me after everything I had done.

Vinh stood alert at the door, "Mai, I really think we should..."

Mai cut him off, "I want to speak to Minh alone for a while, please go and check on the children."

With that, Vinh left the room and headed upstairs.

Mai would get us two mugs from the cupboard; she sat down across from me and poured the steaming water from the kettle into our cups full of tea leaves. Mai sipped her cup while I left mine cool.

I spoke first, "Mai, I hoped that you received my letter, I immediately regretted what I said to you that day."

As I poured my heart out in front of Mai her face softened. Tears began to well up in her also.

She cut me off. "I received your letter, and wanted to write you, but Vinh asked me to leave it alone. You know me and Vinh loved each other long before the day of that incident. Vinh and I already knew we were pregnant before the attack."

All the rumors of Vinh and Mai sneaking off on their walks must have been true.

"But, why didn't you tell me? I was your best friend," I replied.

"I was going to!" Mai exclaimed. "Right after the attack, I visited you many times, but your mom just kept telling me you were recovering. I assumed you were already going through enough. You had lost your little brother, and it never seemed like the right time to tell you. I also know you might have punched Vinh in the nose if I told you." We laughed.

I was so distracted by our conversation that my tea ran cold.

As we talked more, I told her of my husband and our bedroom time, how we hoped for a son and have yet to conceive one.

I mentioned Po's business, and how my cousin Nguyet now has a baby boy named Duy.

We talked late into the night, and when we reached a point where we couldn't think of anything else to share Mai offered that I stay in the spare bedroom.

The next morning, I woke to a breakfast of congee rice soup and Mai introduced me to her children as Auntie Minh.

Mai's oldest was Anh, her eldest son was Hein, and her youngest boy was Tie.

Each morning, Mai and I would walk her children to school together. During the quiet hours that followed, we wandered through the city—shopping, trying on dresses, and visiting charming tea houses and local restaurants.

One afternoon, Mai picked out a stunning dress for me, embroidered with delicate purple flowers. When I saw the price tag, I gasped.

"This is too much," I said.

"Don't worry," she replied with a smile. "It's a gift for my best friend."

Then we visited Mai's mother and father at their meat stall.

Uncle Hung held me in his arms and said, "Look at how thin you still are, don't worry we will fatten you up."

Aunt Lianne made me something special, *Bun Rieu* (crab tomato soup) and braised pork, a dish made for people reuniting after a long separation.

We talked for hours, Lianne interested in my little girl, and how my mother was.

Hung was interested in my brother Khang and how his bullet wound had healed. He was especially surprised to hear Khang was married.

We talked late into the night, all smiles, and the feeling of Mai's village home, sitting at her dinner table spending the days I did as a child with her family.

The days passed in a blur of laughter and exploration. I began to discover the city that had become so familiar to Mai, the life of our small village slowly fading into the background.

One morning, after sending her children off to school, we drove across town to a fancy restaurant where Mai met up with a group of her friends. The restaurant, a graceful wooden structure, had a koi pond rippling gently at the entrance, orange and white fish gliding beneath floating lily pads. Inside, polished black lacquered tables gleamed beneath the soft glow of hanging lanterns, surrounded by well-crafted upholstered chairs embroidered with delicate floral patterns. The air smelled of jasmine and sandalwood. A breeze drifted in from the open-air patio, where a small garden overlooked the bustling city street below.

The women, dressed like true city girls in elegant silk dresses and perfectly styled hair, welcomed me with warmth and curious smiles. Their bangles clinked softly as they gestured, their voices lilting and measured. They seated themselves gracefully, crossing their legs at the ankle, their posture as poised as the orchids arranged on the table.

I wore my new dress, feeling both nervous and proud, smoothing the fabric over my lap as I took my seat beside Mai. My teacup trembled slightly in my hand, and I hoped no one noticed.

The women chatted with soft laughter and confident ease. They spoke about the latest opera at the theater, a new boutique that had just opened, and a scandalous affair rumored to involve a wealthy rice trader. One woman recounted her recent trip to Saigon, painting a vivid picture of Turtle Lake, its rich fountain, and the way it sat at the center of a lively intersection where street vendors gathered at night selling lotus tea, sweet cakes, and roasted corn. Another leaned toward Mai, admiring the delicate pearls in her hair comb and asking where she had found such an exquisite design

As we chatted over tea, one of Mai's friends, Elenor, lifted her porcelain teacup from the table, and the light caught on a beautiful green jade bangle at her wrist—a piece that looked as though it had been passed down through generations of a prestigious family. It gleamed with quiet elegance, and I found myself staring. Elenor must have noticed. She set her cup down gently, leaned toward me with a curious smile, and asked, "My dear, what is that you're wearing around your neck?"

I was caught off guard, suddenly shy.

Mai immediately noticed and smiled. "Is that the necklace from when we were children? I have mine, too." She pulled hers from beneath her dress, revealing a matching locket.

"They're beautiful," Elenor said softly. "You know, my husband is an engraver. He could inscribe something special on them for you both."

"You would do that?" I asked.

"But of course, my dear. It's nothing at all," Elenor replied kindly.

Mai and I exchanged glances, our eyes lighting up. We spent the rest of the meal tossing around ideas for the inscription. After lunch, Elenor led us across the street and down a quiet block to her husband's shop. Along the way, we passed many high-end stores displaying finely crafted pottery, art, and even porcelain etched with intricate details.

When we arrived, the shop window showcased engraved metal pieces gleaming softly in the sunlight. Inside, a stamping and engraving machine rested on a wooden desk.

Her husband emerged from the back room. "Ah, Elenor, you've brought guests," he greeted us warmly.

"Yes," Elenor beamed. "These are my dear friends Mai and Minh. I told them you might help engrave their matching lockets."

"Let's have a look," he said, gently taking the necklaces in his hands. "These are exquisite pieces. What would you like them to say?"

Mai smiled. "Not sisters by blood, but by choice.—M & M."

"A beautiful inscription," he said thoughtfully. "It'll be a tight fit, but I think I can make it work."

He moved to the machine, carefully calibrating the font and size we selected. Then, with practiced precision, he began etching the words onto the backs of the lockets.

"All done," he said, handing them back to us.

We slipped the necklaces over our necks, letting them rest against our collarbones—tiny reminders of a lifelong bond, of forgiveness and shared memory.

As we prepared to leave, Elenor hugged us tightly. "I once had a best friend I loved as much as I know you two do," she said softly. "You will face many challenges in the future, but always remember, time on this earth is short. Make up quickly, and cherish the time you have together."

Her words brought tears to our eyes, and we promised her we would.

After parting from the craft shop, Mai and I wanted to have a little fun, and Mai knew just how.

On our last night together, we drank a cheap rice wine and wandered the city streets like girls again, laughing too loudly, losing our way. We ended up sitting on the curb, Vinh having to come pick us up. He acted mad but it was the first time the three of us had a laugh together since we were children.

On the morning of my departure, sunlight crept through the bedroom window, warming the floorboards and waking me from my sleep. My head throbbed with the dull ache of a hangover—remnants of too much rice wine and too much laughter.

Mai stepped quietly into the room, her hair still damp, from washing. Without a word, she pulled me into a long, tight hug. I hugged her back just as fiercely, trying not to cry.

Then she reached into her purse and pressed a small cloth bag into my hand—filled with dried roots and teas.

"This helped me conceive all three of my children," she said softly. "Now I hope it can help you, too."

I hugged her again, tighter this time, whispering, "Thank you."

It was such a relief to know Mai and I had reconciled and become best friends again. I didn't want to leave her. But the thought of my daughter waiting for me at home filled my heart with peace.

I stepped onto the train, waved goodbye to Mai, her husband, and their children, and settled into my seat. Between two elderly women, I clutched the satchel on my lap and leaned back.

Most of the ride, I drifted in and out of sleep, dreaming of Mai and me as little girls, laughing and playing by the river. I dreamed of our children—Lan and Mai's kids—laughing together in the village fields. And in the distance, I saw a hopeful vision: Mai's eldest son walking hand in hand with my daughter, the two of them grown, perhaps even married.

Wouldn't it be something, I thought, *if our children brought us together once more—this time, not just as best friends, but as family*?

CHAPTER 20

ARRIVING HOME

When I stepped off the train and back onto the platform in our home province, I was surprised by my daughter's beautiful smile. She ran and clung to my leg, "I missed you, Mommy."

I was overjoyed to be home with my husband again. After walking through the market and greeting everyone, my husband and I longed for some time alone.

We returned to our countryside farm for a week to clean and clear the debris left behind from slashing and burning the crops. Our first night home I wanted to try the herbs Mai had given me. I crushed them into a grey mortar bowl and mixed them into my tea.

A feeling of euphoria pulsated in my chest. A warm flush of heat vibrating through my limbs, down to my fingertips, and across my lips. I grabbed my husband and said, "I've missed you—missed our touch, your kiss, all of you."

Next, I bit ever so lightly on his ear, whispering, "Take me."

My husband lifted me up into his arms and laid me on our marital bed. His hands slid down my body like silk. My skin now bare. I felt exposed, embarrassed ever since I had some stretch marks from carrying my daughter.

But he kissed my stomach gently, sinking his teeth deeply into my skin as I twisted and turned in pleasure. His hands caressed my breasts, as he lowered his head further and further, until he was between my legs.

"Enough," I sighed. "I can't take any more of this."

I sat up and gently placing my hands on his shoulders, turned him on his back. I climbed on top of him and we made passionate love.

The next morning, we stayed in bed giggling, kissing, and holding each other close. It felt like our first time.

Later that day, we returned to the fields. The soiled ash had begun to fade. We saw green patches of earth peek through the burnt ground. It was a good sign that our next harvest would be abundant.

But it wasn't just the earth that was healing. My womb had healed, too.

I was pregnant again. Just like that. Perhaps it was Mai's herbs, or maybe her presence—her friendship—that calmed my nerves and brought my body peace.

With the stress lifted, my family surrounding me, and time spent helping Po at his family store, I drifted into a space of happiness and contentment.

I wasn't the only one expecting new life—Khang's wife, Thao, was also pregnant. I was just a few months ahead of her, and we often shared stories of cravings, strange dreams, and the soft fluttering of little feet beneath our ribs.

This birth was much smoother than my first. There were no complications, just the occasional gentle kick from the child growing inside me—a quiet reminder of the life to come. They say boys are easier to carry than girls, and perhaps for me, that was true.

I didn't have the heartburn, indigestion, or nausea like I did with Lan.

I wrote to Mai to tell her that her herbs and teas had been a success.

Mai was overjoyed by the news.

Eight months later, I would bring a baby boy into the world. We named him Cuu.

He had my late father's eyes, my husband's nose, and my mother swore he had my quiet temper, as I had as a child.

Then Thao had her baby, who looked identical to Khang. They named him Bao, and when I looked into his wide, soft eyes, I thought of my baby brother Bo. There was something in the way he watched the world—gentle, curious—that made me feel like a piece of Bo had come back to us.

Time passed quickly. Soon, my son was taking his first steps. Then he began to speak.

My husband never loved anything more than his son. I would watch from the porch as he cradled him in the yard, showing him fireflies at night, pointing at trees and naming the birds and insects.

Everything had finally fallen into place. I had my husband, my children, and my friends.

CHAPTER 21

THE WEIGHT OF QUIET YEARS

War seemed faint and distant during those years. Ho Chi Minh's army had pushed the fighting south, far from our village nestled among the rice paddies and rubber trees. We went about our lives with a cautious sense of relief, pretending the silence of gunfire meant peace.

But we knew better. In Vietnam, silence was just another kind of warning.

It was in that hush that the changes began. Quiet at first. Whispers in the market. Suspicious glances at the post office. Neighbors who once shared tea now barely nodded in passing.

Communism had arrived not with a roar, but with a murmur.

Ho Chi Minh spoke of fairness. Of land to the tillers. Of a Vietnam free from the grip of foreign hands and greedy landlords. But to those of us who had lived through the French occupation, who had built our lives from nothing, the words carried a chill, the fear that what we had earned could be taken and given to another.

Murmurs turned to action, and things began to take a dark turn.

More and more propaganda could be heard over the radio—government officials talking about giving from the rich to the poor. My uncle grew weary and tired of listening to Ho Chi Minh's speeches filled with communist ideologies.

"You can't seriously believe any of his promises," he said.

Then a new official was appointed. He was strict and merciless, a rule follower, loyal only to the party. He and his men arrived in tan, long-sleeved, button-down wool tunic uniforms with pockets on either side, armed with clipboards and lists.

They began documenting everyone's property. Store to store, House to house. They measured land. Counted livestock. Noted who had tiled floors, who had servants, who had electricity.

Our family didn't have much. We had two oxen, a worn plow, and a few small paddies. But even that made us slightly more than average. Enough to be noticed. Enough to make you a target.

My mother answered plainly when the officials came. "We own little, we survive," she said. "Nothing more."

The men noted it down and moved on.

But when they came to Uncle Po's house—the largest in the village, with his well-stocked storeroom, his family rubber grove— they didn't just take notes. They returned days later, asking for records. Deeds. Proof.

Uncle Po spent his life building his rubber tree business. His lands weren't vast, but prosperous enough. He employed local men, paid them better than most, and he stood as a pillar in the town.

My uncle's success had come back to bite him.

They surveyed his lands, carefully counted every rubber tree, checked his acid making process, and looked into any stockpiles of rubber he kept.

After review a slip torn from the official's notebook with taxes, fees, and penalties applied.

The next day the same men showed up at his store in the city. They examined his ledgers and asked about his trade routes. Then they confiscated his receipts and records.

"Temporary review," they said. "A matter of clarity."

Proprietors and local businesses witnessed everything that day.

Slowly, accusations began to stir throughout the city,

"He is a thief."

"He made his fortune off the French."

"He should share it."

These words would reach Uncle's ears.

Once Uncle Po stood a tall man, walking down the street with everyone greeting him. Now people passing him looked away, just as they did my father before being forced inside the French prison.

He laughed at first. "What nonsense," he told my mother. "They've lost their minds."

But then he stopped going to the market, he avoided the tea shops.

The accusations were vague, but they hinted at my uncle supplying the French army.

Uncle Po was trading goods all across Vietnam, and the south was still under French rule. It could have been considered treason if found aiding the enemy.

For military vehicles to transport troops they needed rubber tires. The accusation that Uncle Po was supplying tires was preposterous, the ledgers documented every factory he shipped to, but without them, he couldn't refute such claims.

I wanted to shout in the street at people, have they forgotten, our family as much as anyone's despised the French. My father a victim of their cruelty.

We had hoped for freedom and independence from the French but this wasn't it.

Eventually, land reform arrived.

It began in the North in 1953, when the Party decided to take from the wealthy and give to the poor. It was inspired by China, where similar reforms had reshaped villages through force and fear. In our village, they formed a tribunal—neighbors, mostly. Men and women who had once eaten at Uncle Po's table now sat in judgment.

In the courts, some confessed names to protect their own. Others used the moment to settle old resentments.

We feared what might come next.

One night, I saw Uncle Po pacing. His shoulders hunched, sweat across his brow. He didn't speak, even when my husband offered to help.

"These men," Uncle Po muttered, "they don't want equality. They want to erase everything we built."

He was right.

Within a week, men like him—men who had helped neighbors, who had donated to schools, who had employed half the village—were being called landlords, oppressors.

I felt the earth shift beneath my feet. Not from bombs, but from lies disguised as justice.

Uncle Po surprised us all by throwing a feast. His wife made braised pork and sticky rice. The air smelled of cinnamon and lime leaves. The children played outside while the adults drank tea and laughed—too loudly.

I noticed the bags in the corner. Carefully packed. Folded shirts. Silver coins. Photographs.

After dessert, my mother and Uncle Po disappeared into the

back room. I stayed with my husband and brother, and the women and children. But I could overhear their soft conversation in the next room.

Uncle Po said, "I've thought long and hard about this, and it's the best decision for me and my family."

Mother, "Are you really sure this is the only way?"

Uncle Po paused, "I have a friend in the south who will help us. Things are taking a dark turn here, and I am unsure if I will be able to keep my business."

That day I watched closely as Nguyet's son played with my daughter. I knew what was coming, a long goodbye. Nguyet and I had bonded so much over the last few years, and it was difficult to let her go.

But what could I do, her father's accusations, the tribunals, I wanted for her and her son to be safe. We said our goodbyes, told each other we would write, and they mentioned they were heading South to Saigon.

Later that night, Uncle Po would drive us back to the village, the roads were quiet, the stars unusually dim.

The children, Quang, and I stayed that night at Mother's.

Uncle Po stepped inside his childhood home, extending his hand touching the doorframe, kissed my mother's forehead, and handed each of us a rolled-up bundle of *Dong* (Vietnamese money).

Uncle Po said, "When I get settled, I will send word."

He bent down to my children and group hugged them, looking back up into my eyes, "Take care of them."

I walked to the car and wrapped my arms around Nguyet. We had grown so close these past few years, and I didn't want her to go. But I understood—she was chasing a better future for her son, Duy.

"I love you," I whispered. "Be safe."

Even as I said it, I wasn't afraid for them. Nguyet had come a long way from her childhood days of being scared of ghosts, and crying when Mai chased her. Nguyet had grown into a lion of a mother—fierce, protective, unshakable. If the world was going to change, it would be because of women like her—half laughter, half fire. She didn't just carry hope in her eyes; she carried the will to make it happen.

As we stood in mother's doorway, we caught the last glimpse of Uncle Po's car leaving the village. Inside it carried Uncle Po, Aunt Tam, Nguyet, her husband Long, and little Duy.

Days later when we returned to the market, Uncle Po's doors were shuttered. It would take two months before the government would claim it as their own. Another five to determine how to divide up the land to several families. It took years for the new owners to understand the soil, to learn the harvest. By then, the land had lost its name. It was no longer Po's Grove.

Without her brother's hired hands, Mother left the fields turn to grass. Eventually she would lease out the parcels to other farmers to plant and cure the rice seeds.

Each morning, she came to our home before sunrise. She packed rice and salted fish. She walked the children to the creek, where they splashed in the shallows while she watched from a rock, humming old lullabies.

Mother would always cook a meal and have it ready for us by midday. She passed the time babysitting, often taking the children to play in the creek.

I could tell she was lonelier after Uncle Po left. She had spent her whole life tending others—her children, her fields, helping Uncle Po at his store. Now, with fewer responsibilities and more silence, her spirit seemed dimmer. But she kept herself busy, pouring her love into my children.

One afternoon, I watched from the kitchen window as she showed my daughter how to fold a tiny boat from a banana leaf. They knelt by the water's edge and launched it together, clapping when it floated.

For a moment, Mom smiled like she used to.

The land reform changed our country, but this—the creek, the children's laughter, the soft voice of my mother—this was what we fought to keep.

CHAPTER 22

THE SECOND INDEPENDENCE

The following year, March 13th, 1954, the Battle of Dien Bien Phu began.

France was trying to sever Ho Chi Minh's supply lines. In every village that got the newspapers, men huddled around and read aloud, their fingers smudged with ink, hope and anxiety in their eyes.

"If Ho Chi Minh wins this battle," Quang said, "it could be the end of French rule."

For two months, the battle ensued. Word reached us that a General named Võ Nguyên Giáp led the resistance. Stories said he'd hidden artillery in mountain tunnels, launching ambushes firing the guns and pulling them back underground before French planes could strike.

I was surprised that year because my belly grew like a watermelon out of nowhere. I was already five months pregnant that March. I know I missed my flow a few times, but I really didn't feel any motion sickness at all.

Then, the news arrived: France Surrendered.

Quang clung to the radio in our kitchen looking for an update each day, and he smiled saying, "Maybe our child will be born in a free Vietnam."

It was May 7th, 1954.

We heard it through the crackle of the radio—an old set we borrowed from Uncle Po's store before it was shuttered by the state.

I had just finished cooking dinner. I wiped my hands on my apron and stepped into the main room. Quang was hunched over the radio, fiddling with the dial.

Our two children—Lan, now 11, and Cuu, 7, sat cross-legged on the bamboo mat. Their eyes were wide, faces glowing in the dim light of the oil lamp, and a little one still growing inside.

Static.

Then a voice broke through:

"...the victory at Điện Biên Phủ...a triumph for the people of Vietnam...Ho Chi Minh declares our nation's independence from colonial rule!"

Quang let out a shout and clapped his hands together. "We did it!"

Lan covered her mouth in astonishment. Cuu leapt to his feet, mimicking the soldiers he'd seen, marching around the mat with invisible rifles. Even my baby kicked in my belly. I stood still, the sound of that announcement wrapping around my ribs like a tight embrace.

Ho Chi Minh and that general were hailed as heroes.

Not since the Japanese surrender had our village felt so alive.

Neighbors poured into the central clearing, bringing home-made rice wine, drums, and firewood. Under the moonlight, a fire blazed, and we gathered. Women sang Quan ho folk songs. Men passed bottles of *rượu nếp* and cheered every time Ho's name was shouted. Children ran barefoot, chasing one another, shouting slogans in unison.

Quang stood near the fire, raising his cup. "For the land, for the people, for Vietnam!"

I watched from a few steps back.

I remembered the last time we celebrated like this—in September 1945, when Ho first declared independence after Japan's fall.

That freedom had lasted mere months.

"Twice now," I whispered to my mother, who stood beside me. "Twice, he has given us freedom."

"And twice," she replied, her voice low, "we paid dearly."

In her face, I saw the memory of my brother, who was shot and almost died fighting in Ho Chi Minh's army. Also, of Po who fled south. And we must not forget the neighbors who turned enemies against their neighbors during the tribunals.

But still, the fire burned.

And in that moment, just for a little while, I chose to ignore my fears.

The next week brought more festivities. The city held a parade unlike any I had seen. Our family rose before dawn to take mother's ox cart. When we arrived, flags of red and yellow danced in the air like fire. Truck beds rolled by, packed with veterans in olive green, their rifles slung over their shoulders. Women tossed lotus petals from balconies. From the rooftops, children waved banners.

Quang lifted Cuu onto his shoulders. Lin stood with her hands cupped around her mouth, cheering until her voice cracked. I held my belly, which was about to burst, as my eyes scanned the soldiers, the officials, the new banners reading: "Land to the Tillers," "Victory for the People," and "Independence for Vietnam."

The slogans echoed ones I've heard before—just before my uncle Po's rubber farm was taken. I had watched as officials questioned him, seized his ledgers, and accused him of aiding the French simply for trading across provinces. He vanished the same night he hosted us for dinner.

Now, standing among a sea of faces flushed with joy, I felt the divide in my chest. I wanted to believe in this moment. I wanted my children to inherit a proud country. But the ghosts of past lingered inside me.

Quang turned to me, grinning. "Isn't this what we've dreamed of? No more foreign rulers. No more bribes to corrupt French officials. Vietnam for the Vietnamese."

I nodded, slowly. "Yes...it is what we've dreamed."

But inside, I wondered how long a dream could last before it soured.

That night, back in the village, another fire was lit. Elderly men recited poems from the resistance days. Quang sang a revolutionary song with his arm around a neighbor. I sat by the fire, watching the flames curl upward, trying to warm the chill that had settled in my spine. Then my water broke.

I called out to Quang; he hurried me home. Laid me down on our bed, and the midwife came. It was too early she said, the baby would be premature. She couldn't guarantee a safe delivery. All Quang and I could do was hope for a healthy child. It took hours of pushing and passing out, until finally we heard cries echo through our home.

I had the tiniest little baby boy, who we named Thanh. Thanh born the year of the horse, the year our nation was free.

My husband looked to a bright future.

Ho Chi Minh had indeed brought us independence—twice.

But this second time, it came not with surrender, but with war and plans. Plans that divided families, marked neighbors, and measured worth not in sweat or honesty, but in ideology.

I smiled. I clapped. I celebrated for my children.

But my eyes remained open.

CHAPTER 23

THE WEIGHT OF INDEPENDENCE

Ho Chi Minh had won independence, but the conditions of the French surrender included a painful compromise: Vietnam would be divided at the 17th parallel. Two states emerged—one led by Ho Chi Minh in the north, the other under the rule of Bao Dai in the south.

Still, Ho spoke passionately of "One Vietnam" under one flag. He reminded the people of what had happened in Korea in 1948—how it was split, how families were torn apart. He refused to let the same fate befall our homeland.

To prepare for the struggle ahead, Ho knew he would need to strengthen and sustain his army.

In the weeks that followed independence, our village hummed with talk of reform and renewal. Young men of military age began to appear, moving from house to house. They were polite, even friendly, but they carried notebooks and asked too many questions—about land, about family history, about political loyalty.

One morning, Quang came in from the fields, sweat on his brow and a serious look in his eyes.

"There's going to be a village meeting," he said, setting down his hoe. "They say the Party is coming to redistribute land. It's supposed to be fair. Transparent. Everyone will get what they need."

My stomach twisted. "Like what happened to my uncle?"

"That was a mistake," Quang said gently. "They admitted it. A misunderstanding."

I muttered, "Well, if it was a mistake, shouldn't they try to fix it?"

I wiped my hands on my skirt and looked out over our modest field. It wasn't much, but it was ours. And whatever happened next, we had to hold onto it. No matter what.

At the meeting, Party cadres stood before the villagers and outlined the new policy. Landowners were required to declare any new holdings. Fields were re-measured for accuracy, and redistribution would follow, to ensure fairness and equality. Most villagers nodded. A few even clapped. But I noticed the tight lips and cautious eyes. No one wanted to seem resistant.

After the meeting, two officials approached us.

"Your family owns two hectares, correct?" one asked, glancing at his notes.

"Just under," Quang replied.

"Very good," the man said, smiling in a way that didn't quite reach his eyes. "We appreciate your cooperation."

I stayed silent.

That night, with the children sleeping and the crickets humming outside, Quang and I sat beneath the stars.

"Do you really believe they'll help us?" I asked quietly.

"I believe," he said, "that it's better than what we had before."

I thought of my uncle—how people looked away when he walked past, how the fields went unplanted, how my mother watched the children instead of working the land. Power moved softly, like smoke. But it could choke just the same.

"Let's hope," I whispered.

In the days that followed, inspectors came. The village was surveyed, fields measured, names recorded. The people grew more cautious and anxious in the words they shared with others in the market, on the rice paddies, and within the comforts of their own home.

But for the moment, I kissed my children goodnight, tucked Thanh beneath the mosquito net, and lay beside Quang, the weight of the country resting softly against my chest.

Tomorrow we would work the fields. Tomorrow, the sun would rise over an independent Vietnam.

With each passing day, the children grew stronger. Soon they were all helping in the fields. Mother no longer needed to watch them, but she often visited the land where we worked, offering quiet advice. Her fingers were bent with age, but her mind remained sharp—she knew the soil like no one else.

Weeks later, more officials arrived. Not as conquerors, but as organizers. They carried party pins and polished smiles. They asked similar questions. How many employees each farm had? How many buffalo? Had they attended revolutionary meetings? Are they party members?

Studying us to see if we were loyal to their cause.

Still intoxicated by independence, many villagers answered eagerly. Quang was among them, offering his time and energy to help build a new Vietnam. He believed in it. He believed this was the beginning of justice, that centuries of oppression would finally be swept away.

But I remained cautious. I remembered similar men from the year before—and how innocent people's names had turned into fearful whispers.

I kept busy with the rice, the children, and my mother. But at night, I listened as Quang spoke about "re-education," "redistribution," and "building socialism."

Then came the land surveys.

They came with ropes and sticks, pacing out our lives in strides, as if freedom could be quantified in square meters. My mother's land was small—but it didn't matter. We were family, they said, and had to choose: Quang's farm or my mother's. Ours had better yields, so the decision was made for us.

My mother's land—where she had buried both her husband and her son—was taken. It was plowed to grow food for the army.

We offered to take her in, but she refused. She chose to stay in her family home, which, by some mercy, the government left untouched.

We were lucky. As the tide of tension rose in the village, my mother lost only her land—not her life.

A new tribunal formed. Names were read aloud. Accusations followed: collaboration with the French, hoarding, greed. Some families fled. Others vanished without a word.

Each morning, I rose before dawn to cook, tying my farming hat tightly beneath my chin. My mother arrived soon after with sweet potatoes and kept watch over the children while I worked.

One afternoon, as the sun dipped behind the hills, I walked home and saw my daughter Lan kneeling beside her grandmother at the creek. Thanh at my hip and Cuu splashed nearby in the shallows.

I paused.

This—this moment—was why I smiled during the parades. This was why I celebrated.

Because for now, we were still whole. Still together.

But hadn't the government taken enough already? How much more could be asked of us?

The reforms pressed on. New slogans were painted on the village walls. Weekly meetings were held in the schoolhouse. Those who didn't attend were quietly noted.

Quang remained hopeful. He believed these were temporary sacrifices on the road to justice.

I remained watchful. I had no choice.

Our second independence had come.

Now we would see what might grow in its soil.

CHAPTER 24

THE RED DAWN

By the summer of 1955, the promise of independence had begun to tarnish.

I first heard the whispers at the market—quiet murmurs under breath as women bartered for fish and men smoked under the banyan trees.

"They took old man Binh last night."

"He only had two fields."

"They said he underreported his harvest."

At first, Quang dismissed the stories. "There's always talk," he said. "Old grudges stirred up by change."

But then the soldiers came again. Not in pairs this time, but by the truckload.

Young, clean-faced men in service dress patrolled the roads. They knocked on doors with lists in hand, escorting families to the schoolhouse where the investigative hearings took place day and night.

I watched from my field as our community changed. No one sang anymore when they worked. Children stopped playing in the creek. Even the old dogs seemed to bark less.

At a meeting one evening, a man was dragged to the front. A

former landowner. Not rich, but respected. His face was swollen from a beating, his hands bound.

"They say he underpaid his workers," Quang whispered.

I turned to look at him. "Who says?"

Quang hesitated. "The committee. They have evidence."

"Like they had evidence about my uncle?"

He didn't answer.

That night, the man was taken behind the meeting house. Three sharp cracks echoed through the valley. No one spoke of it again.

A week later, another family vanished. I began to notice the pattern—those who had once employed others, or who had larger plots of land, were the first to go. But it wasn't just the wealthy. It was anyone who asked questions, anyone who hesitated, anyone who was remembered too well.

Quang sat on their porch one evening, staring at the darkening sky.

"We fought the French," he said quietly. "I thought that meant something. I thought we'd be united after the war—that things would be different. But this new government...it's just robbing us. And killing anyone with the sense to stand up to them."

I sat beside him. I didn't speak. I only reached for his hand, interlocking his fingers with my own.

The children were asleep inside. Thanh murmured in his dreams. Lan clutched a yoyo beneath her pillow; one my mother had purchased her when walking the market. Cuu had begun asking me what "re-education" meant.

I didn't know how to explain it.

The next day I sat down to vent my worries to Mai, and began to write.

Mai,

I hope your family is well. I am sure you have celebrated our victory in Hanoi just as much as we have. Much has happened that I need to share. My children will be put in school to learn and get a formal education. Mother unfortunately had to give up her lands during the reunification. We are all wishing you good spirits and hope the tides change into better days as we progress as a free nation. But I worry change won't come soon enough.

-Minh

Quang was already out in the fields working that day but when he returned home, he noticed a red X painted over Mr. Kein's fence. Mr. Kein was an elderly neighbor of ours, and Quang went to report what he saw.

He told the local officials. They said it was likely children playing. But Quang knew better.

Then one morning, as he prepared to leave for the fields, he found a man hanging from the tree near the river.

It was Mr. Kein, our neighbor, and friend.

Quang helped cut him down.

That night Quang was home early.

"You didn't go to the party meeting?" I asked. He explained that he found Mr. Kein. Then he embraced me and whispered in my ear, "We need to be careful. Villagers are now killing neighbors over rumors. This...this isn't what I thought it would be."

I only held him tighter, and together we sat through the long silence of our home slowly being erased.

Before the sunrise a man arrived, clothes soaked with dew, mud on his sandals, hair wild.

It was Mr. Le someone I had known since childhood. He had once been my father's friend, a quiet man who owned a modest but productive patch of land outside the village, where mangos and jackfruit grew in tangled rows. He paid fair wages, lent buffalo to poorer neighbors, and hosted Tet celebrations that lit the valley with music and firecrackers.

"They came last night," he whispered. "My cousin confessed under pressure. They know I delivered fruits to the city hall when it was run by the French. They'll call it collaboration."

I pulled him inside, ushering him to the back where the children still slept.

"Why can't they just leave the past in the past?" I said. "It's been months since the French left. We all aided them, willingly or not. If we didn't help, they forced us."

But it didn't matter.

Regardless, in this new order, he was a "landlord"—an exploiter. A target.

"They'll be here by afternoon," Mr. Le said, his voice trembling.

I looked to Quang. His face was pale.

"We can't keep him here," Quang said quietly.

"I know," I replied. "But we can't let them take him either."

That afternoon, while Quang joined the field crew to avoid suspicion, I packed a small bundle of rice, dried fish, a bamboo canteen. I wrapped it in old cloth and tucked it into a satchel. Mr. Le waited in the small shed near the banana grove.

At dusk, I led him through a dry ravine behind the village, where the brush was thick and the paths old and forgotten. The sun bled into the horizon like a wound.

We said little. There was nothing to say.

After nearly an hour's walk, we reached the tree line where a cart track began—one that led through the hills toward another province. If Mr. Le could stay un-seen he might reach the next town. From there, who knew?

As I said goodbye, Mr. Le grasped my hand.

"Your father would be proud of you," he said hoarsely.

I nodded; eyes hot with unshed tears. "Stay alive. That's all I ask."

He vanished into trees' shadows. I stood alone for a long time, listening for dogs, voices, or worse. But the night held its breath.

When I returned, I scrubbed my hands raw and sat in silence while the children ate. Quang watched me, his face drawn.

"If they find out…" he began.

"They won't," I interrupted. "He's gone. And that's all anyone needs to know."

But the danger clung to me, cold and sharp. I slept with one eye open, always.

The next day, soldiers came asking about Mr. Le. I kept my face blank, my answers short. So did Quang.

Later that evening, when the officials left, I finally let myself exhale. I looked at Quang and saw the recognition I'd been waiting weeks for: he looked at me not as a woman to protect—but as a partner. An equal in fear, and in courage.

Outside, the red banners still hung. The soldiers marched.

But inside, something had changed.

I had found my true allegiance—not to parties or flags, but to people. To justice.

I would receive a return letter from Mai.

Minh,

Things have been difficult since independence. Vinh had to give up his business because he was accused of trading with the French. We are moving, please don't write to this address again. We have been informed government spies are reading the mail. Stay safe…Please destroy this letter for your family's safety.

Mai

Spies reading our mail. I told Quang, he was shocked.

Three days later a knock came—sharp, deliberate, and too early for a casual visit.

I froze mid-step, my heart thudding. Quang glanced at me from the rice pot, then quickly wiped his hands. Outside, the rooster crowed once. The knock came again.

I opened the door slowly.

Two soldiers with rifles hung over their backs.

"Comrade Minh," the older officer said with a nod. "We'd like to ask you some questions. May we come in."

My fingers dug into the doorframe.

"Do you know the whereabouts of Mr. Le?"

Quang said, "He hasn't been seen for several days; we heard rumors he fled during the night."

"Some say he was seen near your house. Near the banana grove."

I kept my voice calm. "He's my father's old friend. He used to bring fruit for the children, but that was long ago."

The younger officer leaned slightly forward, "Mind if we look around?"

Quang's jaw tensed. "Of course not."

They entered, their footsteps thudding heavily on the bamboo floor. The children stirred from their mats, blinking in confusion. My mother sat silently in the corner; her eyes narrowed.

The officials moved slowly through the rooms, opening baskets, tapping floorboards, lifting cooking pots. I stood motionless, the letter...I could hear my heart pounding in my ears.

A soldier picked up the envelope its contents inside, he inspected the cover but placed it back down without opening it.

When the soldiers completed their search and left, I immediately pitched the letter in the fire to burn it. I watched as the flames curled its edges, ink turning to ash.

I couldn't risk them finding anything—anything they could twist into proof that I was against them.

That night, after the children slept, Quang and I sat in our bedroom. No fire, no light. Just silence between us, and the ache of what we now knew.

"I was wrong," Quang said finally. "I thought Ho would bring us peace. I thought this would all end in pride."

For now, we could only pray and hope something would change.

CHAPTER 25

THE GATHERING STORM

A week later, our community gathered for another "People's Assembly." This time, there were no firecrackers, no music, no laughter. Just the sound of bamboo chairs scraping the dirt as families sat in front of the newly raised platform in the schoolyard.

Three accused landowners were brought forward—men who had once been community elders. They stood with heads bowed, flanked by armed soldiers. One of them, an old man with trembling hands, had known Quang since he was a child. A man who sold Quang's family his parcel of lands.

Now the crowd was ordered to chant slogans of condemnation. "End the oppressors! Justice for the people!"

Quang stood in the crowd; his fists clenched at his sides. I held Lan and Cuu close. Even little Thanh, barely understanding, looked afraid.

Suddenly, a voice in the crowd shouted louder than the rest, calling for punishment. Another. Then another. It became contagious—the whole crowd shouting, "Punish them! Punish them!"

The soldiers stepped forward. One of the accused cried out for mercy.

Lan buried her face in my skirt.

I didn't speak. I didn't cry. I didn't chant.

But I knelt in the dirt and picked up a pebble—smooth and round from the nearby stream. I turned it over in my palm, feeling its weight, its silence.

Then the lever was pulled.

It echoed like a clock tower striking the hour.

All three men dropped, their bodies hanging beneath the gallows.

That night, after everyone had gone home, I took the children to the edge of the paddies.

There, I gave each child a small stone and whispered, "We don't throw these. We carry them. Quietly. Hidden."

I looked into my children's eyes, one by one.

"These stones are hard, like us. They will give us strength when the world tries to break us, we must survive."

My husband stood behind me, silent, one hand resting on my shoulder—steady and grounding.

We watched as the stars reflected in the flooded fields—bright points of light floating on the dark water. No banners. No speeches.

Just the promise to survive.

The rain had come early that year. It slicked the leaves, turned the dirt paths to mud, and softened the edges of the village until everything blurred in grays and greens. I stood beneath the overhang of our modest home, watching as Cuu chased Thanh through puddles, their laughter rising despite the chill.

Inside, Quang was hunched over the radio again. The signal was weak, bouncing between stations, voices flickering in and out like ghosts. He fiddled with the dial until a crackled broadcast from Hanoi broke through.

"...President Eisenhower has pledged continued support for South Vietnam...American aid and advisors...danger of Communist expansion, and a domino effect..."

Quang leaned back, eyes narrowing. I stepped inside, shaking water from my shawl.

"They say the Americans are sending more men," he muttered. "Not soldiers—yet. Advisors, weapons, money. But it feels like a rope being pulled from both ends."

I didn't reply. But I thought maybe things would be safer down South. It's where many of the displaced began heading when they had their lands taken.

I stirred the pot on the fire, the scent of fish sauce and ginger rising. Outside, Thanh squealed as he slipped in the mud.

"Ah," I said, smiling to myself, "now Thanh will need a bath."

For a moment, things almost felt normal.

Since the land reform tribunals, things had quieted—on the surface. The loudest voices had been silenced, the villager meetings less frequent. But a different kind of fear had settled, quieter, like mildew. People watched their words. Conversations ended abruptly when others approached. A wrong opinion could cost more than land now.

That summer, I helped a former landowner escape. An old woman, barely able to walk, whom I hid in the toolshed for three nights. We fed her in secret and sent her off with a cart of straw before the next patrol came through. On the second night, soldiers stopped at our home. I nearly choked on my own heartbeat as one of them asked to inspect our shed. Luckily, Quang stepped forward with a well-practiced smile, "The last patrol already checked it two days ago, turned it upside down." The soldiers looked puzzled, crossed off our names on the sheet, and passed on.

When the cart finally disappeared down the road, Quang squeezed my hand. Neither of us spoke of it again, but from that moment, a shared wariness lived in our silence.

Now, we were watching the world shift again.

Rumors came down from the North. Ho Chi Minh was displeased with American involvement in the South. Ngo Dinh Diem, the new leader in Saigon, was refusing to hold the promised national election agreed upon at the 1954 Geneva Accords. Diem claimed the Communists would manipulate it and that the South was not bound by the accords. In response, the Communist Party hardened its stance. Advisors from China and the Soviet Union visited Hanoi. Men from the village began disappearing—recruited, reassigned, or imprisoned.

Quang and I no longer debated politics. We worked our fields. We taught our children to read, to count, to listen carefully and speak only when safe.

CHAPTER 26

WORD FROM THE NORTH AND SOUTH

By 1958, we began to understand where the missing men had gone.

They had been sent to Laos.

At first, it didn't make sense, why did the soldiers go there? But then we heard whispers about a secret trail, being carved through the Annamite mountains, winding south through the dense jungle. It would carry, guns, troops, and supplies all the way to Saigon. But back then, it was just talk, quiet and dangerous to speak about. What they were building would one day be called the Ho Chi Minh Trail.

North Vietnamese forces had been sent across the border into Laos to assist the Pathet Lao, a communist faction fighting against the U.S.-backed Kingdom of Laos. We heard that the fighting was brutal, and that the Americans were watching closely.

By 1960, the tension had thickened, American planes began dropping military supplies to aid the Laotian government. The CIA, under orders from the Eisenhower administration, began recruiting and training Hmong villagers to fight as surrogate soldiers against the North Vietnamese and their allies.

After Kennedy won the 1960 election, and took office in January of 1961, the Americans armed the first thousand Hmong fighters. It was the beginning of what would later be known as the Secret War in Laos—a war few of us in the villages understood, but one that would shape the fate of the entire region.

The man leading the effort in Lao's was General Vang Pao, a fierce and charismatic Laotian commander who became the heart of the Hmong resistance. Backed by the CIA, he built a secret army and operated from a hidden base called Long Tieng, tucked high in the mountains. It grew into a city, the second-largest city in Laos, though it remained unmarked on official maps due to its secret nature.

His fighters protected downed American pilots, disrupted supply lines feeding the Ho Chi Minh Trail, and guarded remote radar and navigation sites that guided U.S. bombers. The Americans called these outposts "Lima Sites," that the North Vietnamese tried to locate and destroy.

As we were distracted by the events unfolding to the west, we were surprised by a visit from someone who had been living in the South.

One evening, Quang's distant cousin Xuan from South Vietnam arrived at our doorstep, soaked and shivering. He brought tales of American jeeps, military bases near Saigon, Catholic priests receiving land and power, and Diem's persecution of Buddhists and suspected Communists. He warned of something darker—of the North's army trying to sabotage the South, and were planning an armed attack.

I served him tea and listened. Quang rubbed his temples, as if trying to ease some great pressure building behind his eyes.

"So now," Quang said quietly, "we are the enemy to them, too."

"Not yet," the cousin replied. "But it's coming. North and South.

Red and Yellow. Vietnam will be split by more than a line on a map."

The next day, I found my daughter Lan sketching in her book. A flag—yellow with three red lines running parallel. A flag I had not seen before.

"What's this?" I asked gently.

Lan shrugged. "I don't know, I saw it in Cousin Xuan's backpack."

I crouched beside her. I didn't know either.

But to my surprise it was South Vietnam's flag. I tore it up and burned it immediately once I found out. If caught with the symbol we would be severely punished.

But the thought of a safer place was implanted in my mind. I wanted Quang, the children, and I to move South believing that democratic Southern Vietnam would be safer than a Northern communist one.

I spoke to Quang, "I think we should leave, let's take the children and go."

By the end of the year, more men had left the village. Recruited for something unnamed, something brewing beyond the hills. At night, planes passed overhead. Strange lights flickered beyond the tree line. The air itself felt heavier, as if the land knew war was returning.

Quang and I would begin making preparations to leave. We asked the whole family, Khang and Mother to go. If Uncle Po was in the South maybe we would be reunited and find each other. Maybe letters he would send are being blocked by those reading our mail.

Our plans were foiled on Nov. 2nd, 1963, when Ngo Dinh Diem, the nationalist leader in South Vietnam, was killed in a coup.

I had briefly hoped the South might be safer, freer. But Diem's death ended that.

"There's nowhere left," I told Quang, "where a good man can lead without being hunted."

Later that same month on Nov. 22nd, President of the United States John F. Kennedy was assassinated. I was 36 when I heard the news at the village square. Many communists took to the streets in celebration.

I stayed at home with my husband who mourned over the hopes we had of a democratic Vietnam; he believed in Diem and Kennedy. My thoughts, not political, felt a deep ache for Jackie Kennedy and her children. He seemed like a good man who didn't want a war here. He only sent advisors. We decided moving South might be dangerous, and decided to hold out hope a little longer.

But history didn't pause for mourning. While the world reeled from the deaths of its leaders, another life from my past came walking through the storm.

A familiar face appeared at our gate. It was Mai, carrying her three children, soaked and trembling. Her once-elegant city dress was stained and torn, her hair matted, her eyes hollow.

"My God, Mai," I gasped. "Come in, come inside."

Mai's children immediately joined Lin and Cuu; their play un-bothered by the storm of adult worries. But I noticed who was missing.

"Where is Vinh? And your parents?"

Mai sat by the fire, warming her hands. Her voice trembled.

"When I got your letter, things were already bad in the city. Public executions in the square—people cheering, chanting 'Kill them!' All the merchants and store owners were being rounded up. Even Vinh was questioned about his allegiance. He tried to sell the shop, but no one dared buy it. Then his partners disappeared. He closed his doors, but my parents refused to shut their meat stall. They believed in the government. They believed everything would be fine."

She paused, swallowing hard.

"Six days ago, soldiers came. My parents were taken. Vinh wanted me and the children out, said he'd try to get them released. We stayed with a trusted neighbor until we secured train tickets. When the soldiers boarded, I thought it was over. But our names weren't on any list. Everything was in Vinh and my parents' names."

"They took my parents to prison," she whispered, "just for owning a meat store."

I reached out and hugged her. "You're safe now. That's what matters."

Days passed, but no word came from Vinh or Mai's parents.

We shared everything—food, blankets, space. The children slept crowded together, and Mai and I stayed up late whispering about our youth, about my brief visit to the city years ago.

But the past couldn't stay in the past forever.

Eventually, talk turned to practicalities. Mai had lost everything in Hanoi, her property seized by the very government she now appealed to. Quang urged Mai to apply for land redistribution. "The government is giving away what they took," he said. "They won't ask questions." Still, we wanted to be careful and Quang came up with a plan—to apply for land redistribution under Mai's maiden name—hoping the new officials wouldn't connect her to her other life.

Mai hesitated. "It feels like stealing."

"It's survival," I said. "We don't have room for everyone here."

Two days after filing a claim—bending the truth to claim destitution, Mai was relocated into the old house that once belonged to Mr. Le, the man I had helped escape.

She finally had a roof and a bed.

A day later, Vinh arrived.

His face was bruised; his head bandaged. He'd tried bribing the guards. It failed. They beat him and threw him out. He returned the next day, disguised as a poor farmer, and managed to see Mai's father breaking rocks in a prison yard.

"He looked me in the eye," Vinh said, "and told me to take care of Mai. Told me to leave him behind. I couldn't find your mother; they wouldn't let me near the women's side," he sighed.

It was too dangerous for him to come by train, since they were arresting wealthy property owners.

So, he walked the entire distance, avoiding checkpoints by smearing himself in dirt, dressing in rags. No one questioned a poor farmer.

Mai wept quietly; her children nestled beside her. Her parents were gone, but Vinh had made it back.

Like my father, Mai's parents had been taken without reason.

Outside, the rain kept falling.

And somewhere in the hills, the storm gathered strength.

CHAPTER 27

FRACTURED EARTH

August 3, 1964

On the morning of August 3rd, 1964, we woke to word spreading that an American ship had been attacked off the coast—a destroyer, they said. The vessel named the *Maddox*. The Americans were calling it an unprovoked act. The radio barked out a single name again and again: Tonkin.

I turned it off. I no longer trusted words I couldn't see spoken.

Villagers gathered in clusters, arguing whether the attack had even happened. Some insisted Ho had planned it, that he wanted the Americans drawn in. Others said it was a trick, a fabrication to justify invasion.

Quang listened; lips pressed tight. He said nothing.

We both knew what this meant, another war.

In early 1965, the U.S. began a bombing campaign—twenty-six bridges, seven ferries, and North Vietnam's radar, military barracks, and ammunition depots were attacked. President Lyndon Johnson called it Operation Rolling Thunder.

Reports from the South grew more grotesque. Napalm swallowed entire villages. Children returning burned, some with no limbs, if they returned at all. GIs, once described as advisors, were now armed troops pouring into cities, towns, and villages.

I had heard that some children in Saigon pretended to shine American boots, only to detonate explosives hidden beneath their rags.

I watched Lan's hands, so much like my own—careful, calloused—and felt ice in my lungs.

"No fields," I reminded them. "No rivers. No woods. Not even the old shrine trail. Understand?"

The children nodded, though Thanh's eyes darted toward the hills.

A neighbor's boy—just eleven—stepped on a mine hidden beneath a decoy doll. He was killed instantly.

I attended the funeral with my children. The casket was closed. I heard they'd barely recovered the pieces. His mother screamed until her voice gave out, breaking into a dry rattle that lingered long after the service ended.

That night, I sat at the table sharpening kitchen knives—not for protection, but out of habit. A nervous ritual. Something to do with my hands while my mind tried to make sense of what my heart couldn't.

The traps came from all sides. The Vietnamese fighters—the *bo doi*—had grown clever. Bamboo stakes dipped in feces. Swinging logs tied to tripwires. Concealed spike pits. I heard stories of American patrols being swallowed whole, disappearing entirely into the trees and never being seen again.

But it wasn't just soldiers who paid.

Civilians triggered traps, too. Women. Children.

"We have no front line," Quang murmured one evening, watching the horizon glow red. "We are the battlefield."

He no longer praised Ho Chi Minh. Not even in private. Too many disappearances. Too many "re-educations" for families of the wrong background.

I heard of villages executed en masse for sheltering the wrong side.

We lit no more lanterns.

We stopped selling grain in the market.

"I followed him when he chased out the French," Quang said, his voice brittle. "Even when he chased out the Japanese. But now..."

I said nothing, placing a hand on his. I had long since buried my belief that one man could hold a nation together.

Our children were growing in a fractured world, old enough to ask questions but too young to completely understand.

"Are the Americans the bad ones?" Thanh asked once, after hearing a plane scream overhead.

I paused. "They don't belong here. But neither does our leader."

That night, the family huddled together on the floor, the walls rattling from distant shelling. Outside, dust settled like ash. The war wasn't coming. It was already here.

I no longer waited for peace.

I waited for morning.

Once the Americans occupied our city and the surrounding villages, young girls who once worked the fields now headed into the city for work.

Bartenders, waitresses, massages, anything to service the GIs for money; some jobs worse than others. Word spread of women taking multiple lovers, and venereal disease spreading.

The Americans quickly settled into place, drinking beer, eating local food, and trading with my neighbors in the market.

But the city still had its dangers, Viet Cong were still attacking the American troops, almost daily you would hear a crack of a pistol ring out, an American solider would drop clutching his waist from being shot in the stomach.

Even bombs would be planted in buildings where American soldiers congregated like the floating restaurant, the local bars, and the police station.

We could see the Americans growing tired of the senseless attacks, and fear and animosity grew.

I kept my children close. Forbidding them from going to the market.

Mai and I allowed supervised playdates inside our homes. It gave us peace of mind and gave the children space to be children, even as the world outside tightened its grip.

Lan often played with Hein. At first, I thought she'd prefer Anh—she was older, more thoughtful—but their age gap must have been too wide. Hein and Lan, on the other hand, acted like best friends. They'd chase each other barefoot across the tile floor, laughter echoing through the house. Sometimes, they practiced tying bandages on each other's arms with strips of old fabric. Once, I found them building a first-aid station with couch cushions and an upturned laundry basket, carefully arranging pots as "medicine" and washcloths as gauze.

I knew it wasn't normal child's play—it was what they were witnessing all around them. But it brought them joy, and I couldn't bring myself to take that away.

As the war escalated, both our families clung to small rituals. We wrote poems. The children—Lan, Thanh, Cuu, and Mai's little ones—sang songs Mai and I had once sung together as girls. Anh, being the oldest and with the steadiest voice often started us off.

One was a French melody, translated into Vietnamese:

"Dưới trăng em múa tay,
Gió nhẹ ru tóc bay..."

Under moonlight, our hands sway,
The wind gently lifts our hair...

We no longer listened to Hanoi's broadcasts. Instead, we listened to our children's breathing as they slept—soft, steady, fragile.

One night, I laid beside Quang, my eyes tracing the lines in the ceiling above us.

"Our children were born into a new Vietnam," I said.

Quang nodded. "But not the one we dreamed of."

The dry season brought no relief. Dust clung to the crops, and the air hung thick with something no rain could wash away—fear. My fields, once my pride, now bore scars of war. Cratered edges, singed stalks, and in the distance, the unmistakable silhouette of a downed American plane, half-buried in jungle overgrowth.

I didn't let my children travel to school for over a year.

"You'll study from home," I told them. "Your books will feed your minds better than rice ever could feed your bellies right now."

Lan, now nearly a woman, along with her newfound best friend Hein, resented the confinement. Cuu, always curious, had taken to sketching planes and tanks in the margins of his schoolbooks. Only Thanh remained quiet, his thumb sometimes drifting to his mouth out of habit, his eyes always watching the sky.

CHAPTER 28

MAI'S HUSBAND

Then came more changes. American forces were expanding. With their jeeps, translators, and loudspeakers, they occupied public buildings and searched for educated locals to assist their operations. Vinh, bitter by how the Viet Cong had treated his family, applied.

He was hired.

Though his initial work was clerical, translating documents, assisting communication, his status rose quickly. The Americans appreciated his fluency and willingness. They offered him and Mai a guarded apartment in the city. It wasn't home, but it felt safe. It felt secure.

The American soldiers worked with the citizens rather than stealing from them.

A sense of safety blanketed us, we felt Vinh's position protected us. I allowed my children more visits to the city, hoping for the tides to change.

Soon, Vinh's role expanded. The Americans asked Vinh and Mai to accompany them during village operations. They were given scripts—talking points about freedom, safety, and the evils of Communist policy. The Americans came bearing sacks of rice, milk powder, and medicines. They played music from speakers and held community meetings where they showed colorful pamphlets and dubbed films showing American prosperity. Children were given candy. Farmers were offered tools and promises.

But these gifts were not without a price.

Soldiers would sweep through the villages after these goodwill events, conducting searches, gathering intelligence. Those who cooperated were marked. Those who resisted were labeled sympathizers.

Vinh stood before crowds and spoke of liberty, of peace, of a future protected by American strength.

"Americans are not here to steal your freedom," he'd say. "Only to protect it from those who would use fear and bombs to take it."

Some villagers nodded. Some spat in Vinh's face. Others said nothing and watched. Vinh didn't flinch when people spat, he stood tall and proud, wearing his civilian clothes with a U.S. issued patch.

For Vinh's assistance the generals liked to hand out incentives to Vietnamese civilians aiding their cause, small things like sacks of rice, soap, or, in Vinh's case, movie theater tickets for his family.

The movies were colorful, and it was a distraction for our children. Quang and I began taking the kids to theaters to forget about the harsh world we lived and to be captivated and lost, if only for a little while by the beauty on the screen.

Weeks passed as the soldiers continued their patrols in the surrounding jungle. If weapons or supplies were found, villagers were taken for questioning. Some returned. Some didn't.

Then we heard automatic weapon fire on the ridge I used to climb as a child to reach the rice paddies my parents once owned.

The Americans had discovered tunnels, and an intense firefight erupted. Vietnamese fighters, AK-47s in hand, emerged from hidden holes, ambushing the platoon.

Wounded men were carried into the village on stretchers. My husband and I did what we could, pressing cloth to wounds, tying makeshift bandages. Helicopters thundered overhead, shooting into the mountains. Soldiers popping red smoke signaling they had wounded, directing the choppers where to land. My husband and I carried some wounded, put them on the chopper, and watched as they were lifted into the sky being rushed to medical tents. In the minds of others', we were helping the enemy, but my husband and I didn't choose sides, if we had to choose any side we chose the side of life.

The firefight lasted from day into night. At night Quang and I sat inside our living room holding our children in our arms. Outside the battle raged, we feared stray bullets might shoot into our home killing us. I went to the window to look out. Phosphorus flares were shot into the sky to illuminate the jungle. We saw movement, shadows moving between the trees. Muzzle flashes and red tracer rounds as shots rang out. I quickly shut the window and went back to my children to protect them.

Silence returned just after 2 a.m., when the fog blanketed the hills.

At sunrise, we heard grenades detonate. The Americans destroying what remained of the tunnels.

What we didn't know then was that Tuan, the young boy who came to me at night to bring me to my wounded brother was among those hiding in the tunnel. I guess treating my brother Khang that day made him want to be a medic. In the tunnels he had a makeshift medical tent, treating injured Viet Cong fighters.

My mother saw him crawl from a hidden exit, dazed and bloodied near her home.

He clutched her arm, begging for help. Mother didn't hesitate, he helped her son, now it was her time to return the favor. She led him to our family house, undressed him, burned his blood-soaked clothes, and gave him fresh ones that Khang had left.

Just after noon, American soldiers returned to our village—more aggressive, shouting, shoving us into the square. With them came Vinh and Mai.

This time, Vinh didn't speak first. A captain barked in English. Vinh hesitated, then translated. "Why are you aiding the enemy? Good men died today."

The captain grabbed a little girl, pressed a pistol to her head. "If you don't point out these soldiers among you, I will kill her."

The square fell silent. Vinh shook, his mouth trembling. The captain screamed: "Translate it!"

Vinh did.

The girl's mother and father sobbed, pleading. Her elderly grandfather ran at the captain, shouting. The captain shot him through the chest, and he collapsed to the ground. The little girl screamed, "Grandfather!" The pistol returned to her head.

"NOW! WHO?" he roared.

The mother searched in the crowd, begging anyone to come forward.

Then she pointed at Tuan. Her voice cracked, "I saw him. He came out of the tunnels. That woman helped him."

The captain turned. "Translate."

Vinh, paused.

"I said translate, god damn it!"

Vinh translated.

The little girl was thrown to the ground. Her mother and father crawled to her, scooping her into their arms, trying to provide whatever false sense of safety they could.

The captain turned his sights on Tuan and my mother. He ordered Tuan to stand. My mother clutched his arm. The captain pistol-whipped her to the ground.

The captain shouted. "Stand!" Each time Tuan tried to stand he was kicked back down to the hard dry earth.

When the captain finished kicking Tuan he finally rose to his feet. The captain pressed his pistol against Tuan's temple and squeezed the trigger.

A single shot rang out. Tuan fell.

My mother shouted, and the captain jumped back in fear, swung his gun aiming directly at her.

I stood preparing to run to my mother but Quang clung to my arm stopping me. Mother looked into my eyes shaking her head no. Then she looked at the captain and before she could say another word a bullet passed through her forehead and exited out the back of her skull.

I screamed.

The soldier turned toward me, toward my children, with gun in hand. I braced for the shot.

"Enough!" Vinh cried.

The captain's hand shaking from his shot nerves. He lowered his pistol.

"Torch the village," he said loudly.

Soldiers lit the tips of their flamethrowers and began burning down the village, going home to home, lighting each on fire until they were all burning. But they hadn't finished yet.

About six soldiers, grabbed four girls. Children leapt into the well to escape the chaos. A soldier pulled a grenade pin and dropped it in.

Eight children hiding in the well were blown into pieces.

The captured girls were dragged up the hill.

I saw the trees move. I heard their cries. I looked to Mai. She wept, but said nothing.

When the captain shouted, "Let's go!" Mai and Vinh followed.

How could this happen, after everything, Vinh reassuring us that the Americans were here to protect us. Our small sense of security was completely shattered in front of our eyes.

They executed my mother. They are raping women and killing children. I went back into my darkest days being reminded of what the Japanese did, raping me and Mai and killing my baby brother Bo with a bayonet. I fainted.

I woke in my husband's arms back at our home, I couldn't speak, I had no energy to even lift my hands. The sight of my mother being shot in the head kept flashing in my mind. *Why? Oh, why did this have to happen to me?*

Then my sorrow turned to anger, Mai and her husband Vinh, they let this happen. They are responsible for this.

Three days is how much time the village had to mourn, each day that passed became harder and harder to bear the truth. I tried to pretend it didn't happen, but heart-broken parents crying into the night, the candle vigil laid around the remnants of the well, and the coffins sitting outside the artisan's house, made realizing the facts unavoidable. The villagers gathered the dead. In total Tuan, my mother, eight children from the grenade in the well, and one of the girls who resisted being raped had been murdered.

My mother gone, women raped and children murdered.

My mother joined the tree where my father and baby brother were laid to rest.

On the day we laid the victims to rest, the families gathered together constructing a bamboo raft, not to carry their bodies, but to carry their memories. The victims had already been buried in quiet, private ceremonies. This was something else. A vigil. A farewell.

Each family placed something on the raft: a child's toy, a piece of jewelry; for my mother we laid a photograph of her and a *Khan Dong* or elegant neck scarf she wore with her *ao dài* (long dress). We placed the items into a box.

Khang and Thao were there. Thao stepped forward and gently placed a small bundle of butterfly pea flowers on top of the box. The blossoms, with their deep indigo hue, symbolized rebirth, motherhood, and a spiritual connection to the divine.

We stood in silence, watching as the raft floated down the river. A candle, fixed carefully at its center, burned low—its flame flickering in the distance. When it reached the patch of hay we had laid, the raft caught fire, burned softly before sinking beneath the surface, leaving only ripples behind.

It was an emotional moment for Khang and I, both our parents had been taken too soon.

But I could never forgive Mai for what happened. I was traumatized for months. The nightmares wouldn't let me rest. I couldn't close my eyes without seeing my mother fall to the ground with blood pouring out. Sleep became a stranger. Peace, a memory.

The Americans had come with smiles and candy.

And left as monsters.

CHAPTER 29

THE INVITATION SHE COULDN'T BEAR

The days after I returned home from my mother's village passed in a fog. The house seemed quieter than usual—not because my children were silent, but because I could no longer hear them through the ringing in my ears. Sounds came muffled and strange, like I was under water. The image of my mother's lifeless body returned every time I blinked. The smell of burnt village ash clung to my skin no matter how often I bathed.

I no longer went to the market. I couldn't even bring myself to wash the rice, to stir the broth, to feed my own children. It was Quang who rose early, bundled the children's clothes, combed Lan's hair with his thick fingers, and gently persuaded our youngest to eat just a few bites of sweet potato.

I sat on the porch most days, watching the chickens roam, my arms slack at my sides. The weight to move them too heavy as grief settled into my bones like humidity—thick, immovable, suffocating. I did not cry. The tears had long since dried. What I felt in my heart was a quiet, festering rage.

I thought often of Vinh. Of how his uniform looked the day I saw him standing beside those Americans. How he saluted them. How he shook their hands. How could he still wear their military dress—stand next to them, like a loyal dog—after everything they had done?

And Mai—sweet, foolish Mai. My once-dearest friend. The woman who had held my hand through childhood, who had shared rice when times were lean, who had promised me that the Americans would bring safety, fairness, modern life.

I wanted to scream.

The engraved locket we both carried I tossed to the floor, I told my husband to destroy it.

I wanted to hate Mai with every fiber of my being—but that hatred tangled with love in a way I couldn't unravel.

Late one afternoon, while folding the children's clothes, Quang paused and looked over his shoulder. "There's something I need to tell you," he began.

I glanced up, eyes tired.

"A letter came today," he said, slipping a crumpled envelope from beneath his sash. He had tried to hide it in his shirt, but it had fallen out while bending. I snatched it before he could explain.

The paper trembling in my hands as I read the words. My breath caught.

An invitation.

A formal request for our presence at a banquet in the city—to honor Vinh's service, to pin a medal on his chest. A celebration. A ceremony.

I crumpled the letter in my fist.

"How dare they," I hissed.

Quang reached for my arm. "Minh, I didn't want you to see it—"

"How dare they invite us, Quang! After what they did? After what he did?!" My voice cracked, sharp as shattered porcelain. "You should have burned it!"

"I was going to," he admitted. "But I thought maybe... you'd want to know."

"I won't do it. I won't go—not for either of them."

Later that week, Mai came. She stood at the edge of the farm with a broken smile, holding a small cloth bundle of mango slices for the children. I didn't greet her.

"I heard about the letter," Mai began, carefully. "I—I didn't know they would send one. I wanted to tell you, Minh. About Vinh. About what he's been doing. It's not what you think—"

"You think some medal makes it better?" I snapped, my voice low and bitter. "You think some ceremony will make my mother rise from the dead?"

Mai's lips trembled. "No. Of course not."

I stepped back, my shoulders rigid. "Don't come here again. And don't bring your children to play with mine."

Lan's voice quivered behind me. "But Mom...I want to see Hein."

I turned sharply. "Be quiet. Go inside."

"But Mom—" she cried.

"I told you to go inside!"

Lan ran off, sobbing.

Mai's voice broke the silence between us. "They're just kids, Minh. They don't know the weight we carry. Maybe they can be what we couldn't."

I turned and walked back inside, slamming the door behind me.

Mai left soon after.

That night, Quang held my hand as we laid in silence.

"You don't have to forgive them," he said. "But don't let it eat you whole."

I didn't respond. I stared at the ceiling, thinking of the smoke curling through my mother's roof as it burned, of the future my children would live in—one I no longer understood.

And somewhere deep inside, beneath the layers of grief and fury, a single thought flickered—maybe one day...but not yet.

CHAPTER 30

THE SECRET RESISTANCE

The monsoon season rolled in with its familiar rhythm: rain tapping against rooftops like impatient fingers, swollen rivers creeping up muddy banks, and gray skies hanging low as sorrow.

I no longer kept track of the days.

But Mai did.

She returned to the village once more, despite my warning. This time she didn't bring mangoes. She came with something heavier. Something that made her hands shake as she clutched a folded sheet of paper to her chest.

I spotted her from the kitchen window. She nearly turned away—but Quang met her eyes and gave a small nod, his way of asking her to try.

Reluctantly, I opened the door.

"I won't stay long," Mai said quickly, before I had a chance to speak. "But you deserve to know the truth. About Vinh."

I folded my arms across my chest, skeptical. "What truth could possibly change what I saw with my own eyes?"

Mai unfolded a sheet of paper, careful not to let the drizzle soak it. "This is an article—from an American newspaper. It mentions our village."

I gasped and snatched the paper from her hands. My eyes raced over the opening lines:

> *A decorated South Vietnamese commander is under investigation for war crimes in central Vietnam. Multiple witnesses. A cover-up exposed by a whistleblower within the ranks...*

I looked up, heart pounding. "What is this?"

"It's Vinh," Mai said softly. "He's the whistleblower."

I stared at her, stunned into silence.

"He wasn't who you thought, Minh. He risked everything. He documented every wrong—every raid, every girl stolen from her family."

She stepped closer, voice low. "For years, he's been collecting information. Sneaking documents, hiding them under floorboards, copying ledgers and lists of names. He sent them through an American reporter who visited the base. If the commander had found out, they would've executed him."

I clutched the paper tighter, my fingers trembling.

Mai's voice cracked. "Everything happened the night your mother died. I found Vinh at the kitchen table, hunched over scraps of paper, copying names in the dark."

"If they catch you—" I whispered.

"Then let them," he said, eyes blazing. "We can't survive by pretending we didn't see what we saw."

"I didn't stay with him just for love," she continued. "I stayed because...in a place where every candle had gone out, he became the light. I wanted to be proud of him, Minh. But all I felt was terror. Every night I slept with our children curled against me—and a knife under my pillow."

Mai's eyes shimmered with urgency. "The trial is real. It's happening now. People from all over the country are watching. The commander was arrested. So were the soldiers who..." She swallowed hard. "Who hurt, those girls. Even the one who threw the grenade."

She took a breath. "Vinh got all their names. He gave them everything. They're even considering the death penalty."

I sank down slowly, as if my knees could no longer bear the weight of what I'd just heard.

"Minh, you can watch the trial live, Vinh has access to the base, the trial is being aired live on AFVN-TV (American forces Vietnam network)."

Mai handed me a pass, "I hope they pay for what they did." Her head sunken low as she left.

The next morning, I would wake my children up in the early morning light. I dressed them and told them we are going to the market. In Hue, I made my children cross the street every time I saw an American soldier, afraid, I wanted to avoid them. Outside the military base gate, I paced back and forth for 20 minutes. Until my youngest son said, "Mom, it's hot out here, when are we going to find some shade?" Once I snapped out of my daze, I approached the gate and handed the officer the pass, he lifted the gate and allowed me to walk though.

We went to the nearest building with a TV, the mess hall. Dozens of American soldiers and Vietnamese citizens sitting with eyes glued to the screen. There I saw two familiar faces, older now, but it was Beni and Kiet. They now worked at the military base as chefs. I never imagined they would end up as cooks. When they saw me, they came to express their sympathies.

"Your mother was an amazing person, Minh. We were so sorry to hear the news," Kiet said.

"We are always here if you need anything," said Beni.

Each day they would watch the trial with me when they could, as they took turns working in the kitchen.

Six American soldiers standing trial on the screen, being asked to take the oath, "swearing to tell the truth and only the truth" of the events of that day. I watched without so much as a blink, clinging to my purse, as the story was retold in detail. I never wavered.

For days, it was the same routine: get the kids up, wash, walk the path to Hue, hand the guard my pass. The trial went from days to weeks. It was my reason for living, without seeking justice I had no purpose.

Sometimes, I spotted Beni and Kiet in the back kitchen of the base canteen, wiping sweat from their brows and cracking jokes as they served stew to grumbling Marines. We'd exchange tired nods—our only comfort was knowing that we still had each other to depend on.

The villagers would shout at the screen, waving their hands in disgust, but so were American troops. They shouted things like, "Hang them." I never thought American soldiers would support the Vietnamese people. I guess they weren't so evil after all. The few caused my hatred toward the many.

Finally, after two months, the trial's verdict was read. My brother's wife came, and my children and husband were there supporting me.

The verdict was read:

"The massacre that occurred at Long Dong Village on March 3rd, 1967, involving the rape of four women and the murders of 11 men, women, and children, the court hereby finds you guilty. The verdict is as follows:

Private 1st Class: Mitchell Spalding

Private 1st Class: Benjamin Erikson

And Corporal: Drew Cummings

"You are found responsible for participating in the rapes at Long Dang and will receive 10 years minimum with a 12-year maximum sentence.

"Private 1st Class: Thomas Bellows you are found guilty of the rape and murder of An Ma Li and are sentenced to a minimum of 12 years with a maximum of 14 years in a military prison."

I didn't know An Ma Li, but I saw her in myself, in Mai, in the scars we didn't dare name out loud.

I was fifteen again. Riding my wagon into the city. Japanese soldiers had dragged Mai and I out of the cart throwing us to the ground. One laughing as he tore my tunic. My brother Bo screamed for them to stop. One of them silenced him with a bayonet through the chest.

I clenched my purse tighter, knuckles bone-white. I could still feel his blood in my palms.

"Sergeant 1st Class Kane Wilson you have been found guilty of throwing a grenade into a well hiding innocent children and will receive a 15-year minimum with a 20-year maximum sentence for the murders you have committed."

As I heard those words, "children," "well," "grenade"—a cold wave crashed over me.

I was no longer in the cafeteria. I was back in my village, standing before the stone rim of that well, watching as little bodies were pulled out in pieces. I could smell the smoke, hear the shrill cries of mothers collapsing to the earth.

I remembered the tiny sandal one child had worn—it had landed near my foot, scorched at the edges but still pink. I had picked it up and screamed so loudly Quang had to hold me down to stop me from tearing at my own face.

"Next, Captain Michael Williams, you are responsible for the shooting deaths of two villagers Linh and Tuan; furthermore you are responsible for the entire massacre that took place at Long Dang Village as you were the commanding officer at the time of the event. You will receive a minimum of 20 years in a military prison with a maximum of 30 years."

People cried out and wailed in the mess hall when the verdict was read aloud. My husband squeezed the back of my shoulder saying, "It isn't enough, but at least it's something."

I didn't speak for a long time. My fingers rested on the edge of a piece of paper I was crumbling.

Although my hands trembled and I was still upset that they didn't receive the death penalty, I rested easy knowing that everyone in the room around me was just as angry at the verdict. For the first time, I didn't feel like I carried this burden alone. Both American and Vietnamese alike were shouting in solidarity against the verdict.

Thao said she was sorry that Khang couldn't come, but he was needed at the docks. She added, "He won't be happy with the outcome." Then she took my hand, "Minh your mother...she'd want you to live your life, and not dwell on the past."

As Thao left, I wondered how she'd break the news to my brother. I knew he would be furious—just as I was drowning in grief.

The next day, Mai stopped by to share the results of the trial, but I was still not interested in what she had to say.

"Minh, I miss you, I know you might not be able to forgive me, but Vinh did all he could to punish them. After the trial, they took away our apartment. Stripped Vinh of his rank. He's back in his father's old furniture shop now. Making tables with his bare hands."

I imagined Vinh in dusty clothes, sanding planks of wood while his children calling to him from across the market—the same market where he first fell for Mai, where they all once laughed before the world fell apart.

"It doesn't erase what happened," I whispered.

"No," Mai said gently. "But it's a start."

My grief was not yet gone, but it was momentarily suspended.

"I still hate him," I said. "I still don't know if I can forgive you."

Tears rolled down my face as I looked up at Mai, who I hadn't allowed myself to look at directly since that day.

"I don't know if I can ever forgive you, but I definitely cannot forgive Vinh."

Mai reached out, wrapping her arms around me as I wept on her shoulder.

"Just go," I said. "Please leave me."

But Mai just held me tighter. "I know you think I'm no better than those men," guilt in her voice. "I ran when you needed me most. I left you to face everything alone, when I should've been at your side."

I wept in Mai's arms for what felt like an eternity.

For now, at least some small part of me felt justice had been given.

That trial meant so much to our fellow villagers and to me.

Soon, however, it would fade in the distance as another much larger scale massacre would occur.

Another commander, by the name of Lt. William Calley, entered a village on a search and destroy mission. The village name My Lai (known to Americans as Mai Lao). Over three hundred civilians would be massacred. Twenty-six soldiers would be charged. Only Calley would be convicted.

He was found guilty of murdering 22 villagers and initially sentenced to life imprisonment. Appeals led to a reduced sentence. Calley's sentence was later reduced again to 20 years and then further to 10 years, due to appeals and public pressure.

The shock of that trial shook our village, like they had forgotten the devastation it caused all those families.

I suppose they had already made an example out of our trial. And with the American government under mounting pressure for drafting young boys, they wanted to be lenient on the war crimes these young men were committing. We heard stories and saw photographs of Americans opposing the war.

Young men sitting, waiting in their homes, watching their TV screens waiting to hear if their birthday would be selected. If selected, they had to report for duty and would be enlisted and shipped to fight in Vietnam. Often those selected would try to use medical issues to avoid selection, burn their draft cards, be enrolled in college, or flee to Canada to avoid the draft.

In America, thousands gathered on the Capitol lawn, holding up signs and chanting, "Hell no, we won't go!"

At least we knew some Americans stood by us.

CHAPTER 31

NOT MY DAUGHTER

The summer rice harvest came early that year, the heat drawing every last drop of sweat from the workers' backs and turning the paddies into gold-tinted mirrors. Life had slowly found a rhythm again in the village. I was still cautious and quieter than before, returning to tending my garden, selling vegetables on weekends, and trying to ignore the way grief still hummed beneath my skin.

I noticed Lan, my daughter, had started spending more time at the market. She insisted on going alone now, her basket of rice on one hip and a spark in her eyes that I hadn't seen since my own childhood. I didn't question it much; after all, Lan was a teenager. But Quang watched our daughter with knowing eyes, the kind a father uses when he sees a secret unfolding before anyone else does.

It was at dinner one evening, when I was alone with Quang, the kids were still out gathering water at the well. I sat silently chewing the sticky rice I made earlier in the day, when Quang said casually, "Lan's been seeing Mai's boy."

My chopsticks dropped mid-air from my hands onto the floor.

"What did you say?"

Quang sipped his tea. "They're not children anymore. They talk at the market. Walk together sometimes. Just wanted you to know."

I set my bowl down. "You knew? And you said nothing?"

"What harm is there in two young hearts?" Quang said gently. "They're kind to each other."

I pushed back my chair, appetite gone. "Not him. Not Vinh's son, I won't let her."

That night, I couldn't sleep. I tossed under the mosquito net, my thoughts a jumble of confusion and betrayal. The idea of my daughter with his son was unbearable.

I needed air.

I stepped outside, letting the breeze cool my skin. The moon was full, casting silver light across the path that led to the river.

And that's when I saw two silhouettes of people speaking in the distance.

As I approached to see who was speaking, I hid myself behind a tree.

It was my daughter Lan and the boy—Mai's son Hein—walking slowly, side by side, near the edge of the village. They laughed quietly, his hand brushing against hers. As they neared the front gate, he leaned in and kissed her. A gentle, uncertain kiss.

My heart twisted.

I stepped out from the darkness like a storm breaking.

"Get away from her!" I snapped, voice sharper than I meant it to be.

The boy startled and stepped back. Lan turned in horror.

"Lan! You think I wouldn't find out? That you could sneak around like a thief?" I yelled, pointing at the boy. "You are not welcome here. Not now. Not ever."

Lan stepped in front of him, her voice trembling. "Don't talk to him like that."

I stared at her, stunned.

"You think you can talk back to me?" I forced.

"He's not his father," Lan said. "You don't even know him. He's kind. He listens. He makes me laugh."

"He's Vinh's son," I spat.

"And I'm your daughter!" Lan cried. "But you're so full of hate you don't even see me anymore."

We stood there, mother and daughter, locked in a war neither of us wanting to fight.

"You go to your room this instant Lan, and for you, go home to your mother Hein."

That night, Lan cried in her room. She refused to speak to me.

Quang found me sitting on the porch later, my hands clasped tightly together.

"She hates me," I said flatly.

"No," Quang replied. "She's just young. And she's in love."

"You know she talked back to me," I muttered, still stunned.

Quang gently placed his hand over mine. "You know she got that fiery side from you."

I didn't answer. I couldn't—not without admitting he was right.

He smiled softly, then added, "You once told me you wished you and Mai could've been sisters. Maybe this is life trying to give you that gift—through them."

I swallowed hard. "Anyone but him. Anyone but Vinh's boy; I've barely begun to even forgive Mai, and now my daughter is dating one of their children."

Quang smiled faintly. "He's not Vinh. He's just a boy who loves our daughter."

I sat in silence for a long time, watching the shadows of the trees sway across the fields.

Maybe it was the breeze. Maybe it was Quang's quiet patience. But something inside, began to thaw.

"Do you think," I whispered, "this is how my mother felt—watching me fall in love?"

Quang squeezed my hand. "Probably. Except she wasn't as scary as you."

I laughed despite, wiping my teary eyes.

For the first time in a long while, the future didn't seem like a battlefield.

"I'm willing to give this boy a chance." I said.

That night as I readied myself for bed, Quang came into the room. He said, "I've been holding onto something for you."

"What is it?" I asked.

Quang pulled out the locket of Mai's I had thrown to the floor.

"I know you asked me to destroy it, I didn't know if it was the right time to return this, but I thought…"

I stopped his words. "Thank you," I said.

I didn't wear it but I didn't throw it away either. For now, I kept it by my bedstand and would hold it in my hand reading the inscription, to calm me.

CHAPTER 32

WHEN THE RAIN WOULDN'T STOP

January 1968 should have been the dry season. I knew the rhythm of the land well—January and February were supposed to bring dust and cracked fields, not the slow, bone-soaking rains that clung to rooftops and turned the land into rivers. But the rain fell anyway. Day after day, like the sky itself had forgotten what time of year it was.

January 31st, 1968. The first shots rang out around our home, which would become a major battleground for the next month. Unknowingly, the Vietnamese army had amassed over 100,000 soldiers. Their mission: to recapture our city of Huế. The Americans, well-established and dug in, would fight street by street trying to keep the city from being captured. This event would be marked in history as the Tet Offensive, but for my family and the civilians living through it, it would be remembered as the Huế Massacre.

I stood barefoot in the dim room of our home, rain pouring down outside, when I saw a soldier emerge from the surrounding woods. But it wasn't just one—thousands of North Vietnamese troops emerged from the tree line. I was at my window looking out at the rain with Thanh when they came. I froze. Never had I seen so many soldiers at once. More than I'd seen even during Ho Chi Minh parades. They moved silently across the mud, water buffalos dragging mortar cannons behind them.

I clutched Thanh in my arms, motioned for Quang to come to the window. When he saw the mass of soldiers, he signaled to the children to go to their rooms and stay down.

Luckily, the troops passed through our village without harming a soul. Their target was Huế.

They went up the hills and into the mountains disappearing into the fog, then we heard the screams.

Screams and whistles blowing, a high-pitched piercing sound, signaling "ATTACK." We knew the Viet Cong were around us, hiding in their bunkers and tunnels, cracking off a few shots at American troops on patrol. However, my husband Quang and I never expected this. For the next month our lives would be forever shaken. It didn't feel like just a battle; it felt like the entire war was at our doorstep.

In Huế, the Americans were dug in well, moving freely in the streets, mostly undisturbed by the sporadic fighting that had broken out over the years. Bombs sometimes shook the market, landmines blasting in the fields. We had grown used to the sounds of distant gunfire. But this was different. Dozens of battalions, four full regiments of North Vietnamese soldiers, were now outside our village.

Huế the third-largest city in Vietnam, with its 140,000 civilians, 15,000 American soldiers, and 30,000 South Vietnamese combatants became a battlefield overnight.

After the soldiers passed our village, the shelling began. Mortar after mortar lit up the skies. For a full month, we listened to the whistle and crash of explosions, to the rattle of gunfire that never ceased. The children couldn't sleep. Neither could we.

We stayed indoors. I forbade the children from leaving, no matter how stir crazy they became. No market. No farming. The city was a death trap, and their lives were all that mattered.

Rumors trickled in. Families killed. Streets littered with bodies. The NVA and VC pushed deeper into Huế, executing anyone linked to the South Vietnamese or the Americans—teachers, clerks, monks, mothers. Several American chaplains, stationed in the city to offer spiritual support, were executed in cold blood.

I also heard about Goong, a Vietnamese monk who converted to priesthood during the war. I knew him since I was a small girl—gentle, kind-hearted, compassionate, and deeply devoted to his faith. He used to bring a wagon around town to collect food donations and stored them at his church, then distributed them to families suffering from famine and the brutal tolls of war. He was among the dead. Killed by the North Vietnamese, seen as a traitor who was aiding the American cause. I could never understand how someone could kill a man of the cloth, no matter what his faith.

Several Vietnamese civilians who had worked with the Americans—clerks, translators, cooks, even janitors—were rounded up. I worried about Kiet and Beni since they worked on the American base. I met many people at the base when walking each day to watch my mother's trial unfold on the cafeteria television. Now many were missing, presumed dead.

I didn't know what had happened to Mai, her husband, or her children. Each day I braced myself for news. I told Lan I'd heard they were safe, hoping it would keep her from running off to search.

We even limited the radio to avoid scaring the children. Reports of casualties of war were broadcast each day. Even my husband struggled to listen to it.

As the battle raged, the rain kept falling. Trucks sank in mud. Roads vanished beneath water. One of our neighbors, a secretary to the four-star American general in command of the Huế forces, whispered a name: Operation Popeye. American planes were seeding clouds with silver iodide and lead, trying to wash out Vietnamese supply lines. But the storm they summoned turned against everyone. Trucks disappeared into sludge. Water clogged drains. People walked through waist-high water. Even solid roofs collapsed.

Quang and I reinforced our roof with bamboo and tarps, bolted the windows, sealed the doors. We built a pit beneath the house, just wide enough for the children to slip out the back of the house if anyone threatening entered.

"If I say run," I told them, "you go, and don't look back."

"Even if you don't come?" Cuu asked.

I didn't answer.

Every pot in the house caught water. We were soaked constantly, the floors soggy, but we were alive. Quang tried to lighten the mood, placing his cup beneath the roof's leaks. "At least we don't have to walk to the well," he joked. We laughed, but not loudly.

At night, we stayed quiet. Gunfire cracked. Sometimes there was a knock. We didn't answer. Once, soldiers tried the door. I held Thanh against me until their boots faded into the distance.

We passed the days reading books to the children—the ones my father once read to me. It gave them a rhythm. It gave us all a reason to breathe.

Then came the napalm.

It was dropped from the skies above the tree line near our village. The jungle exploded into flame. Men ran, covered in fire, screaming as the sticky fuel clung to their skin. The heavy rains offered no mercy—it couldn't put them out. I will never forget the sight of them—walking, stumbling, their bodies lit like torches.

One child in our village, a girl of just seven, had her legs burned in a napalm blast. When her family found her in the rubble of their collapsed home and tried to lift her to take her to the hospital, the meat and skin on her legs slid off the bone into their hands. She let out one final scream and instantly died right there, in their arms.

That was what the war had become.

It was too dangerous to go to the city. But then Cuu fell ill.

For three days, I told myself it was nothing. Just a cold. Children got sick all the time.

The first morning, Cuu pushed away his bowl of rice. "My throat hurts, Ma."

I felt his forehead. Warm, but not burning. "Rest today," I said. "You'll feel better tomorrow."

But the next day, he wouldn't leave his sleeping mat. His breathing sounded different—shallow, like he was trying not to disturb something fragile in his chest.

On the third day, the fever came.

His skin burned against my palm. When I tried to give him water, he turned his head away, too weak to drink. Lan brought him a flower she'd picked from near the window, but Cuu's eyes stayed closed.

That night, I sat beside him listening to his breathing grow more labored. Each breath was work. Each pause between breaths lasted too long.

Quang found me there at dawn, still holding Cuu's hand.

"How long has he been like this?" he asked.

"It's getting worse," I whispered.

We both knew what that meant.

A high fever. His skin was hot to the touch, and his cough rattled like dry rice in a tin can. He hadn't eaten in two days. His eyes turned glassy and unfocused. At night, he pulled at his blankets in delirium. During the day, he shivered in a sweat-soaked haze.

Quang begged the village doctor to come.

One look at our boy and the doctor shook his head.

"Pneumonia," he said.

I tried to stay calm. "What can we do?"

He sighed. "Nothing I have will help. He needs penicillin—from the city. All I can do now is give him herbs for the cough."

The village doctor left us with nothing but fear.

"Pneumonia," he'd said, and the word hung in the air like smoke.

For two days, we watched our son fade. His cough turned wet and rattling. His lips took on a bluish tint. When he tried to speak, only whispers came out.

"I have to go to the city," I told Quang on the second night.

He was mending a hole in the roof, trying to keep busy. His hands stilled on the bamboo.

"Minh, no."

"The medicine is there. The American pharmacy—"

"You could be killed walking those streets."

I watched him work, his movements sharp with frustration. "And if I don't go?"

He set down his tools. "We'll find another way."

"What other way?" my voice cracked. "What other way is there, Quang?"

He couldn't answer.

"It's too dangerous right now," he told me. "They're shelling day and night. We don't know who's bombing who anymore."

We argued. I pleaded. He shouted, "Enough!"

I felt hopeless in that moment, not knowing what else to say or do.

The next morning, Cuu's breathing became so shallow I had to lean close to his breath to feel it. His chest barely rose and fell.

I told Quang to hurry and get the doctor.

Quang, knowing how severe Cuu's condition had become, left immediately in the rain not even bothering to put his coat on.

With Quang gone, I seized the opportunity, I had already made my choice, in my mind the only option was to get Cuu penicillin from the city.

When he left, I waited five minutes. Then I gathered the last of our coins into a tin. I told Thanh and Lan to stay inside and lock the door.

"Do not open it," I said. "Unless it's me or your father."

I wrapped Cuu in a blanket and kissed his forehead.

"I'll come back," I whispered. "I'll bring what you need."

Then I left for the city.

I told myself: I will not sit by and let my son die while I do nothing.

It was a half-day's journey by foot.

I slipped climbing the hills, my feet sank into the mud like it was quicksand. The rain fell like it had no intention of stopping. The journey took an hour and a half longer than I expected, but I mustered every ounce of strength in my body to push forward.

My feet blistered, and I had tiny cuts, the skin softened by the rain and climbing over sharp rocks with nothing more than my sandals.

By the time I reached the outskirts of Hue, I was soaked to the bone.

The bridges I had crossed as a young girl now lay in ruins, partially destroyed and worn by war. The city once bustling with color in all its grandeur, became hollow and destitute. What was once a vibrant stage of pageantry now felt haunted, its streets abandoned.

The city was in ruins.

Walls blown to pieces by the bombs, littering the street with rubble. Doors hanging crooked on broken hinges. Pools of dirty water collected on the ground mixed with blood. The gutters overflowed with sludge, and rats picked at corpses lying in the streets.

I had never seen such horror.

The smell—rot, gunpowder, burned flesh—made me dry heave. I bent over and vomited into the water pooling near my feet, then swallowed hard, wiped my mouth, and kept moving.

As I approached the pharmacy, I saw them.

American soldiers.

They sat on overturned crates outside a sandbag post, smoking cigarettes beneath an awning of sheet metal. Their rifles leaned nearby. One wore a helmet covered in cartoon drawings and had an ace of hearts tucked into the strap. Another carved his name into the butt of his rifle with a dull knife. A third adjusted a battered field radio, squinting through the static.

When they saw me, they grabbed their rifles.

"Who goes there?"

"I need a pharmacy," I said in English. "Medicine for my son."

They scanned me up and down. Their eyes lingered too long. One finally nodded. "Move along."

I stepped past them, heart pounding.

Then came the voice.

The static cleared, and a woman's voice poured through the radio. Smooth. Calm. English. Vietnamese—but English.

"Good evening, American G.I.s. Are you lonely tonight? Wondering why you're here, in a country that doesn't want you?"

One of them cheered. "She's back!"

"Turn it up!" another shouted. "I missed her last night!"

They laughed like boys at a party.

"Your government tells you lies. They say you're fighting for freedom...but whose freedom? Look around. The children don't smile. The mothers bury their sons. And you—you are dying for a cause that isn't yours."

One held up his canteen. "To Hanoi Hannah—the sexiest voice in Vietnam!"

"I'd defect just to meet her," someone laughed.

"We know who you are. We know your unit. And we know what happened in Da Nang. Johnson from Ohio...we heard about the Dear John letter."

More cheers.

"Go home, G.I. Go back to your mothers. This is not your war."

"You're surrounded on all sides, defeated at Khe Sanh, and your failed operation at Hải Lăng."

I stood in the rain, sandals soaked through, watching grown men hang on the words of a woman who spoke their language but belonged to us.

Then I turned the corner and saw the pharmacy—still standing.

Inside, a man stood behind the counter wearing an American poncho and a sidearm at his hip.

"Penicillin?" he asked.

I held out the tin.

He opened it, counted, and tossed me a box, only a quarter full.

"It's for the troops," he said. "I gave you all I could, don't expect more."

I didn't reply. I wrapped the medicine in cloth and stuffed it inside my blouse.

When I exited, the soldiers were still listening.

"G.I., your government has abandoned you. They have ordered you to die. Do not trust them. Defect. It is a very good idea to leave a sinking ship. They lie to you, G.I. You cannot win this war. Your rich leaders grow richer while you die in the swamp. They'll give you a medal, G.I.…but only after you're dead. G.I., your own planes bomb your own men. The skies are dangerous. Goodnight, G.I. And don't forget to write home to your mothers."

"She's got a point," one soldier said.

"Yeah, but she says that crap every night," another muttered.

Still, none of them turned the radio off. Because her voice was the only one that sounded like home.

I heard distant shots. I checked my blouse, making sure I hadn't dropped a single pill of my son's medicine. I needed to return home as quickly as possible. Remaining exposed on those streets any longer would cost me my life.

So I ran. Sprinting as fast as I could to get away. My only thought was of Cuu, who desperately needed the pneumonia pills I carried. I didn't walk. I didn't stop to breathe. I ran through the flooded streets, past more bodies, past the screams of people calling out for help. I ran until the jungle swallowed the city behind me.

By nightfall, I was home.

Quang scolded me, but the moment he saw the medicine, he rushed to give it to Cuu.

Later, after Cuu was settled and breathing more softly, we sat opposite each other at the table—the oil lamp flickering between us, the sound of rain still steady on the roof.

"You shouldn't have gone," he said flatly.

I met his eyes. "And what was I supposed to do, Quang? Watch our son die?"

"I told you I'd find another way."

"Another way?" I snapped. "With what? While you argued and hesitated, I went."

He stood abruptly, pushing back the chair with a scrape. "You could've been killed."

"I know that!"

His hands clenched into fists at his sides. "You left the children alone. You ran off into a war zone with no one to protect you. What if something had happened?"

"It already was happening!" I shouted, my voice cracking. "Our son was dying. And you were too afraid to do what had to be done."

Silence fell.

His voice, when it came, was low and shaking. "I wasn't afraid for me, Minh. I was afraid for you. I can't—" he swallowed. "I can't lose you, too."

My anger faltered, twisted into something softer.

I stepped around the table, placed my hand on his chest, over the thudding fear he didn't know how to name.

"I know," I said quietly. "But you almost lost me anyway. You almost lost us. If I hadn't gone—"

He pulled me into his arms, so suddenly I gasped.

"I'm sorry," he whispered.

I buried my face in his shoulder and nodded. "And I couldn't bear the thought of losing our son."

"Will the medicine be enough?" he asked.

"I don't know," I said.

That night, none of us slept well. I sat beside Cuu, watching for any sign the medicine was working. Quang checked the doors and windows twice. The children whispered to each other in the darkness.

But by morning, something had changed.

Cuu's forehead felt cooler. His breathing came easier. When I offered him water, he drank.

"Mama," he whispered. It was the first word he'd spoken in days.

I pressed my face into his hair and wept.

Cuu's forehead felt less hot.

Two days later, Cuu opened his eyes. His pale skin had returned to a normal color. His cough lingered for a week but grew weaker each day.

When he laughed again, I wept into my hands.

And then—the rain stopped.

After what felt like weeks of drowning, the skies broke open, and the sun returned.

For four days, we lived in careful hope.

Sunlight streamed through the windows and Cuu sat up to eat broth. He even smiled when Thanh showed him a beetle he found.

The distant sound of shelling continued, but it seemed farther away now. We began to believe the worst was over.

I started rationing our food more carefully, planning ahead. Quang talked about checking on the neighbors, seeing who had survived. We needed to know what was left of our world.

"The water in the well might be contaminated," he said on the fourth morning. "I should check the river."

It seemed reasonable. Necessary, even. The immediate crisis had passed.

"I need to check the well, feed the oxen, and check on the neighbors. I'll be back before midday," Quang said, kissing my forehead. He took the bucket and rope. At the door, he turned back.

"Keep the children inside. Lock the door."

"I will."

"Don't open it for anyone."

"I won't."

He nodded, but didn't leave. Something in his expression made me stand.

"What is it?"

"Nothing," he said. "Just...be careful."

After he left, I watched from the window as he fed the ox, and until he disappeared beyond the tree line. A strange unease settled in my stomach. We'd grown so used to staying together, to facing everything as a family.

An hour passed. Then two.

Thanh kept asking where Papa was. I told him he'd be back soon, but my eyes kept drifting to the window.

I could hear birds calling in the distance, noise of insects in the grass but it felt wrong somehow. Too quiet.

I started lunch early, just to have something to do with my hands. Boiled the last of the rice. Stirred it too much, and kept peering out the window, fearing if my husband will be safe.

"When will Papa come back?" Thanh asked again.

"Soon," I said, but I was starting to wonder myself.

By the time I heard his footsteps, my heart was racing.

When Quang walked through the door, he tried to smile. But I knew something had changed.

He set down the bucket, it was empty, I wondered if he couldn't make it to the river, but didn't want to ask in front of the children. His clothes were muddy. His hands shook as he tried to remove his sandals.

"Quang?"

He looked at me, and I saw something I'd never seen in his eyes before. A kind of hollow shock.

"I'm fine," he said, but his voice sounded far away.

The children ran to him, but he barely seemed to see them. He sat heavily at the table and stared at his hands.

I sent the children to play in the back room and sat across from him.

"What happened?"

He didn't answer for a long time. When he finally spoke, his voice was barely a whisper.

"Bodies," he said. "So many. Floating in the river. I saw VC lining up families along the river and shooting them in the head. Children Minh, younger than Thanh. I was so shaken I accidentally dropped my water bucket and a soldier turned looking in my direction. Fortunately, I hid behind a tree before they could see me. I waited until they passed."

I clenched my jaw. "You have to be careful, Quang. I can't bear to do this alone. Without you I would be lost."

"I know," he said softly. "I know."

Now I understood why he was so worried. I was putting my-

self in just as much danger going to the city a few days ago. Neither of us felt a sense of safety, we were completely at the mercy
of these soldiers. Any second they could take and kill us.

Quang was visibly shaken after what he saw. I could tell he
was more stressed than usual.

That night, I could feel Quang's body tense beside me every
time a sound came from outside. Twice, he got up to check on the
children, moving silently through the house like a ghost.

When I woke in the morning, he was sitting at the table, staring at nothing.

"Quang?"

He looked up, and I saw that the man who had left yesterday
morning was gone. In his place sat someone who understood,
finally, what we were truly up against.

"We can't stay here much longer," he said quietly.

I nodded. We both knew he was right.

The war had found us. There was no hiding from it anymore.

February 24th. Shells pounded closer. The radio reported the
South Vietnamese army was retaking the city. A week later, on
March 2nd, the battle officially ended. The NVA had withdrawn.
But the silence that followed wasn't peace. It was grief.

Lan begged to go into the city to find Hein. I didn't let her. Not
yet.

In the weeks after, the truth emerged. Bodies in gardens.
Schoolyards. Wells. Men found with their hands bound. Children
still in their pajamas. Monks in robes, face down in mud.

We learned that Beni had survived the mass executions
of workers. Whatever list the North Vietnamese used to round
up those accused of supporting the Americans, his name was
somehow not on it. But Kiet was not so lucky. He was captured—

dragged from his home, bound at the wrists, and forced into the line of prisoners being marched into the jungle.

Beni saw it happen. He chased after the soldiers, shouting, pleading, begging for Kiet to be released. When they ignored him, he tried to offer himself in Kiet's place. But Kiet turned back bleeding from a gash on his temple, and shook his head.

"Go, Beni," he said, voice hoarse. "Before they change their minds. Don't be stupid. One of us has to live, get away while you still can now."

It was the last words they ever exchanged before Kiet vanished into the trees with the others. No body was ever recovered. No grave ever marked.

His death stirred emotions inside me—not only with grief, but with a kind of painful clarity. It stirred memories of Mai. I imagined how she might have screamed if it were me being marched into the jungle. I wondered how I would have fought, how I would have broken myself in half, to save her if the roles were reversed.

Many more stories like this would be told.

Huế had 140,000 residents. By the end of the three-week battle, 80 percent of the city was rubble. 7,000 civilians dead, another 2,000 missing. 2,600 American soldiers killed. 9,600 South Vietnamese. And more than 40,000 Northern Vietnamese soldiers lost their lives. Over 50,000 on both sides wounded.

The Tet Offensive was meant to turn the tide of war. It became a massacre. We couldn't forgive the communists for what they did to the citizens of Huế.

They claimed they were liberating us.

All we saw were the dead.

Ho Chi Minh's great push to retake Huế ended in more unnecessary bloodshed. We couldn't forgive him for the destruction and lives lost in the city; it was senseless killing in my eyes.

When we finally reached the city, we discovered that Mai and Vinh's home and business had been spared the worst. Aside from a few shattered windows from nearby blasts, a broken lock—likely from someone seeking shelter during the fighting—and a scattering of mortar holes in the street and sidewalk, the shop stood remarkably intact.

Mai was outside, sweeping glass from the steps. Vinh stood inside counting inventory, while the children rearranged furniture, nudging chairs and wiping dust from cracked tabletops. Relief washed over me. Despite everything, Mai and her family were safe.

Quang walked up to Vinh and clasped his shoulder.

"How did you survive all this?" he asked gently.

Vinh's voice was hoarse, worn ragged by days of silence and fear. "We hid in the basement," he said. "We stayed down there for days. They shelled the entire block. We heard boots marching overhead. We were lucky no one found us. At one point, we ran out of food. Just a little rice left—but I wouldn't even let Mai boil it. I was afraid the scent might attract someone and we would be discovered. So instead of boiling it we ate it dry."

There was a long pause between them, thick with the things that couldn't be said—how close they'd come, how much they'd lost, how fragile survival really was.

When looking at my husband standing there next to Vinh a memory had woken inside of me. I don't know why that memory came back to me just then—maybe because things had been so heavy for so long. But I suddenly remembered the time I visited Mai in the city, long before the war had swallowed us whole.

One night when spending the week with Mai and Vinh, she had a bottle of homemade rice wine hidden behind a stack of laundry.

"I got it from the noodle vendor's cousin," she whispered like we were sixteen again.

"Is it even safe to drink?" I asked.

"No," she said, grinning, "but we're doing it anyway."

We drank it in little porcelain cups. It burned going down and tasted like fermented rainwater. By the third cup, we couldn't stop laughing. We laughed about everything—the price of papayas, our mothers' constant warnings, even the way old men on the street cleared their throats.

At some point, we decided to go downtown and buy sweets. We ended up getting lost halfway between her apartment and the river, arguing about which bridge we needed to take to get home.

Vinh had to come find us.

When he arrived, we were sitting on the curb eating boiled peanuts and singing an off-key version of a song we couldn't quite remember. My hair was a mess. Mai had a peanut shell stuck to her cheek. We must have looked like two escaped farm girls who had no idea what city life demanded.

Vinh crossed his arms. "You know you're both grown women."

"We are," Mai said, slurring just a little, "but we're not that grown."

He looked like he wanted to be mad. He really tried. But when Mai hiccupped and fell sideways into me, knocking over the rest of the peanuts, he cracked. The corner of his mouth curled up, and then he started laughing, too.

He drove us home in silence, but I saw how happy he was looking at Mai.

It was one of the last nights we were all happy together.

As I refocused my attention, that's when I saw Lan spot Hein.

She didn't hesitate—just ran to him and leapt into his arms, her whole body folding into him as if her legs might give out otherwise. It had been over a month and a half since they'd seen each other. I could see the tremble in her fingers where she wrapped her arms around his shoulders.

I decided in that moment not to interfere. They had been pulled apart by chaos and deserved their reunion.

I brushed past them and said simply, "It's time to go. We need to see if anyone is selling anything in the market." Quang and the other children followed.

Lan hesitated, then caught up with us. I turned to her.

"You can stay and help clean up if you want," I said, keeping my voice steady. "Looks like they could use the help."

She froze. Her eyes scanned mine, searching for the catch. To her, it must've felt like a cruel trick waiting to be taken back. But when she saw that I meant it, her gaze softened. Tears welled up.

"Thank you, Mom," she whispered as a single tear streaked down her cheek.

"Go on now," I said.

She smiled, hugged me tight, and ran back to Hein.

Mai looked up at me and smiled, and I gave a slight shrug of my shoulders back. As soon as Lan disappeared behind the wooden shutters of Mai's shop, I took a breath of dust-laden air and stepped back into the wounded heart of Huế.

The city I had once known—the gentle laughter of schoolgirls on bicycles, the smell of lotus tea from old cafés, the shaded corridors of temples where incense always lingered—was gone.

Stone shattered. Roofs split wide open like cracked bowls.

I walked past what was once the imperial library—its ornate roof now half collapsed, scrolls and books scattered like dry leaves. Pages fluttered from branches. A boy with a bloody bandage around his ankle sat at the edge of the rubble, humming a lullaby I hadn't heard in decades.

Near the Citadel wall, smoke still rose. The great gate—once a symbol of power and peace—looked like the broken jaw of a dragon, torn from its hinges.

The Citadel—our pride, our inheritance, the memory of emperors, scholars, poets, and warriors—had been bombed. Tanks had rolled through sacred halls. For weeks, the Red Flag flew from its highest tower. Now it lay in the street, full of bullet holes, tattered and stained.

In the back of my mind I thought, "This was where we knelt to honor our ancestors, it's completely destroyed."

I reached out and touched a scorched temple pillar. My fingertips came away black. A monk's robe lay buried beneath chunks of stone, its edges charred. A prayer bell—cracked, silent, laying on its side.

Even the Huế Railway Station, where Uncle Po used to load freight onto the trains, was not spared. It had been heavily damaged in the fighting. Rail traffic was halted, and even if food or building materials were sent by freight, they would sit idle—stuck until repairs could be made.

The city I had known my whole life now smelled of gunpowder and rain.

In the market, most storefronts were shuttered. Food was scarce. The only things for sale were fried frog legs, a few fish, and bowls of sea worms harvested from flooded soil. Even the

insects had surfaced—earthworms and bugs crawling for breath,
now plucked up by starving families and dropped into pots.

The old Huế had vanished.

What remained was a ghost made of smoke and hunger.

CHAPTER 33

THE NIGHT THE RIVER TOOK HIM

In September of 1969, our dear leader, Ho Chi Minh, died. The whole country cried. Sorrow passed like a cloud over the cities and villages. There were mass funerals held in every city. People wailed and bowed in the streets, their eyes filled with tears, and incense smoke twisted its way toward the heavens.

But for Quang and me, it was not grief we felt. It was something closer to relief.

We knew his cause. We'd lived beneath his socialist vision for years. But we no longer believed in his agenda, not after all the suffering we had seen. We hoped—quietly, cautiously—that the new leader, Lê Duẩn, might steer us toward something better. Toward peace.

We turned inward. We shut out the war and focused on our family.

It was around this time that Thanh grew legs that couldn't sit still. He wasn't so little anymore at fourteen, nearly fifteen, he ran like wind through the fields and across the village paths. He and the neighborhood boys spent their days near the river, hiding in a shallow cave, trying to avoid the boredom that hung heavy in those long, humid days.

Some of the other boys would talk about sneaking out at night and how the cave was much better when the adults weren't watching. They told Thanh that they would light candles, sit around the fire, and share ghost stories, talk about girls, and eat crackers and candies they stole from the market. A young boy's adventurous dream, roughing it with his friends.

They planned to meet there later that night.

I should've seen the signs.

When darkness fell over the village, the night heat thick and humid. Quang and I already in bed. Thanh waiting and listening until our breaths deepened, only then he would sneak out. He slipped quietly across the yard, barefoot and brimming with foolish courage. In his pocket, he carried a matchbox and a single rice cracker.

The moon was low and yellow, hanging like a lantern over the trees.

He didn't hear the voice until he reached the edge of the trees.

"Thanh?"

He turned.

A shadow stepped from behind the jackfruit tree.

It was Hein.

Hein was tall now, twenty-five and sharp-eyed. His hair curled over his ears, and he wore his father's old shirt—patched at the elbow, sleeves rolled.

"What are you doing?" Hein asked

Thanh puffed up. "I'm sneaking out to the cave by the river."

"You shouldn't be out here," Hein said. "Go home."

Thanh crossed his arms. "And what are you doing out here? Visiting my sister, I bet."

Hein's eyes narrowed, but he didn't deny it. "Just go home to bed."

Thanh stepped into the woods. "You can't stop me."

Thanh looked around, a little dazed and confused in the dark, afraid he might get lost, "You better come with me if you don't want me to rat you out to my mother."

Hein gave a long sigh. "Then I guess I'm going, too."

They walked in silence for a while, the narrow path to the river glowing silver under the moon. But something in the air changed the deeper they went. Thanh's bravado slowly melted. The air changed. The frogs quieted. The crickets fell still. The trees held their breath.

When they reached the riverbend, the water was high—too high. The recent rains had flooded the banks, and the current surged violently.

Thanh stood at the edge of the cave and called out to his friends, "Hey, are you guys here?"

No response.

Hein scanned the area, his brow furrowed. "It's too dangerous. Let's go."

Thanh took a step back from the rock ledge, but his foot slipped.

He tried to grasp anything to stop his fall, but the ground was covered in mud and slick moss. He plunged right where the water was deepest. I imagine the sound, his cry splitting the night, and then the splash.

"Help! Help Me!"

He thrashed, arms flailing, choking on water.

But the river didn't care, pulling him deeper. Thanh's head bobbed as it came up to the surface, but as soon as he went to make a sound water rushed into his lungs. His arms swinging violently in a blind panic.

Hein didn't hesitate. He dove in.

Thanh would hit his head on a rock and fall unconscious.

Hein found him, grabbed the back of his shirt, and kicked toward the shore. His lungs burned. His heart pounding. His body shaking from the cold.

He didn't remember how they reached the shallows. Only that he collapsed, coughing, wet, and breathless. Thanh limp beside him.

Hein started pushing on his chest, breathing into his mouth.

Hein shouted, "Come back, Thanh! Come back!" as he did chest compressions.

Minutes had passed, and then, my son coughed. Spitting up buckets of water.

"You idiot!" Hein gasped. "You stupid, lucky idiot!"

Thanh blinked. "You saved me."

Hein nodded, too exhausted for words.

They laid there, side by side, looking up at the stars. Both soaked and shivering, but alive.

Back at home, I was already awake.

Call it a mother's intuition.

I saw Thanh's mat was empty and my heart dropped. I went outside just as Hein was walking up the path. He carried Thanh in his arms—muddy, scraped, but breathing.

I didn't speak. I just took my son and held him close. He was shaking like a leaf.

Quang woke and rushed to my side, kneeling down he checked Thanh's limbs. Nothing broken. A cut on the brow. A bruised rib.

Only then did I turn to Hein. My voice was low.

"What happened?" I asked.

"I saved him," said Hein. "I told him not to go to the river but he did anyway."

"You were watching him?"

Hein nodded. "Yes."

"Why?"

He glanced down, then met my eyes.

"Because I love your daughter and I wanted to make sure he didn't get hurt."

I stared at him. I said nothing for a long moment. "Thank you. Thank God you were there. Thank you for bringing my boy home."

That night I didn't sleep.

I lay beside Thanh, my hand gently resting on his chest, rising and falling with each breath. I couldn't stop touching him. I needed to feel him to believe he was okay.

I let Hein sleep by the fireplace. I didn't have the heart to send him home, not when he was soaked to the bone and had just pulled my boy from death's mouth.

Down the hill, the river kept flowing. Quiet. Relentless. As if nothing happened at all.

But in our house, everything changed.

Hein saved my baby boy, and in that act of kindness, I could fully forgive Mai.

CHAPTER 34

THE CHILDREN OF ASH AND RAIN

The wedding was small—nothing like the elaborate city affairs seen in films or magazines. But it was beautiful. In a quiet corner of the village, beneath strings of paper lanterns and the low murmur of drums, Lan and Hein stood hand in hand, garlands of flowers around their necks and joy lighting their faces.

I watched from beneath a fig tree, my heart full and aching at once. Mai stood beside me, our arms touching, and for the first time in years, I did not pull away.

"They look so young," I said softly.

Mai smiled. "So did we."

Later that year, Lan gave birth to two boys, strong and loud like the river they were born beside. Mai and I took turns holding the babies, rocking them to sleep, sneaking them sticky sweets when their parents weren't looking.

We were grandmothers now—tethered together not just by history, but by family.

But joy lived beside hardship.

The furniture store that Vinh and Mai had reopened after the trial, began to suffer. Inflation, driven by the war's unrelenting hunger, made luxuries like polished chairs and carved cabinets unreachable to everyday people. Customers stopped coming. Materials became scarce.

As I entered my 40s, Richard Nixon came to power. Though he promised peace, his strategy, scorch earth. Cambodia, Laos, and villages like mine were sprayed with Agent Orange and burned with napalm.

Napalm had ravaged the forests in the central regions, blackening trees and scarring the hills. There was no more mahogany, no more acacia. Even bamboo became harder to source. The few delivery carts that did arrive brought word of charred towns and families living beneath tarps.

Then came the Agent Orange.

Sprayed across the fields from low-flying planes, it poisoned everything in its path. The earth itself turned against us. Trees died standing up. Rice paddies withered. Buffalo and pigs dropped dead in their pens. Mothers wept over barren plots of land that once fed entire villages.

My own garden, only received a light dusting carried by the wind, but it was enough to turn it yellow within days. The cucumbers shriveled. The mint died. Even the weeds surrendered.

And the rivers—once lifelines for bathing, fishing, and collecting water—became haunted. American navy boats patrolled them day and night. Along the banks, Viet Cong lay in wait, ambushing them with AK47s. The patrol boats carrying a crew of only four, mounted with twin 50-caliber machine guns returned fire sweeping the banks killing anything in its path. The heavy rounds tore through trees, huts, and human bodies alike—leaving nothing but devastation in their wake.

Children no longer bathed there.

Fishermen stayed away.

Leaving only birds hovering to eat the rotting corpses cooking in the heat from the sun.

With nothing being imported and all the forests being burning around us. There was nothing left for Vinh to sell.

Vinh tried to hold on, moving whatever few chairs they had to the roadside, but there were no buyers. One morning, he sat on the porch with Quang and I, rubbing his temples.

"People used to buy furniture for new homes," he said. "Now they buy rope to tie down tents."

Quang nodded. "Hard to think about tomorrow when today's still on fire."

Yet amid the ruin, family endured.

Mai and I began spending more time together—not out of obligation, but out of comfort. We cooked together, shared news, helped each other raise the grandchildren. On rainy days, we told old stories to the boys, sitting under the awning as water drummed the roof like marbles falling on a tin tray.

Forgiveness had not come quickly. But it had come.

I'd still flinched when helicopters flew overhead. Still woke some nights thinking of my mother, her village, the smoke.

But when I looked at Mai—so tired, so worn, but still standing—I no longer saw betrayal.

Instead, I saw survival.

CHAPTER 35

RIVERBOATS AND PUPPET STRINGS

The furniture shop closed for good in the spring.

Vinh didn't cry when he locked the doors one final time. He stood in silence, key in hand, staring at the empty shelves and the layer of dust coating the windows. Mai touched his back and said nothing—some griefs are best shared in silence.

They moved back to her childhood village soon after, into a modest wooden home Vinh built himself. It sat near a quiet bend in the river, where water lilies floated like resting butterflies. The walls still smelled of fresh timber, and the floors creaked with every step. It wasn't much, but it was theirs.

Best of all, it was close to their grandchildren.

Quang and I welcomed the change. Our families were neighbors now, our homes connected by a dirt path that wound through a grove of bamboo. Most mornings, Mai and I sat on straw mats under a canopy of leaves, our laps heavy with sleepy children and our hearts heavier with memory.

Mai would bring pickled eggplant. I would bring green mango slices dusted with chili salt. The boys, sticky-mouthed and barefoot, darted between the homes, carrying messages, toys, and sometimes frogs.

Sometimes, we all went down to the river with wooden boats carved by Quang and Vinh. The children would float them down the stream, cheering as the little vessels bobbed and turned. I would sit by the reeds, watching the boys run along the banks, remembering another time—long ago.

One afternoon, the village held a harvest festival.

It was smaller than the ones from our childhoods—no dragon dancers, no loud parades—but the spirit was the same. Strings of lanterns glowed above the main square. Stalls offered grilled corn, rice cakes, and sweet tea with tapioca pearls. The air smelled of smoke and sugar.

At the edge of the square, an old man prepared the water puppet stage. A bamboo curtain concealed the puppeteers, and a shallow pond served as the stage. Children clustered at the front, giggling and pointing as wooden dragons, frogs, and farmers danced atop the water.

Mai sat beside me in the second row. Our grandchildren nestled between us, mesmerized.

The show told a simple story—a fisherman losing his net, a phoenix returning it. But I didn't watch the puppets. I watched the way our grandson leaned against Mai's shoulder, safe and content.

I leaned over and whispered, "My parents' first date was a puppet show. My father said he laughed so hard he dropped his rice ball in the pond."

Mai smiled. "Sounds like something Quang would do."

I chuckled. "He once dropped a jackfruit on his foot and didn't walk right for three days."

We laughed—really laughed—for the first time in what felt like years. And as the puppets twirled and the music played, I looked up at the sky turning orange with dusk. I felt like my life was complete.

CHAPTER 36

THE HARVEST AFTER WAR

Years would pass, our families happy and together.

In January of 1973, American troops withdrew from Saigon due to the signing of the Paris Peace Accords. These accords officially ended the U.S. military involvement in the Vietnam War. The agreement stipulated a ceasefire, the withdrawal of U.S. troops, and the release of American prisoners of war. The last U.S. combat troops left South Vietnam on March 29, 1973. It was a great relief to so many in North Vietnam, and celebrated by all in our village.

As America's attentions focused elsewhere, North Vietnam gained military and financial support from Soviet Russia and China. The South Vietnamese Army became more and more demoralized and lost battle after battle. The final campaign known as the Ho Chi Minh campaign was launched on March 10th, 1975. In just 51 days, Saigon would fall.

Leading up to the conflict, North Vietnamese soldiers disguised themselves as civilians, collecting information on troop movements, base locations, and civilian morale. Without American aide the South Vietnamese army was careless in their defenses, they left their flank open, spread their forces too thin, and even allowed an intelligence ship to sail through the navy head-quarters and gather intel on their sea defenses.

It was April 30, 1975.

The radios crackled to life before dawn, carrying the weight of history in every syllable. Across Vietnam, people gathered around dusty speakers and battery-powered boxes, listening as the voice of Lê Duẩn rang out, firm and triumphant: "The war is over! Our country is reunified!"

I stood barefoot in my garden, hands in the earth, tears streaking down my face. Not loud sobs—just quiet relief. My fingers trembling in the soil, not from fear this time, but disbelief.

Peace had finally come, and Vietnam was to be unified once more, communism at that time seemed distant after Ho Chi Minh's death.

For the first time in decades, relief, the village didn't have to worry about waking to sirens or gunfire. No bombs would fall in the distance. No soldiers marching through the fields. The rice paddies shimmered in the early light, untouched and golden, ready for planting.

In the days that followed we saw the newspapers. Photos of helicopters landing and evacuating desperate civilians and U.S. embassy personal to safety during the fall of Saigon. An operation known as Frequent Wind, thousands desperately trying to flee in a crowd outside the metal gates surrounding the Embassy. Even a photo of the first North Vietnamese tank entering the Presidential Palace at approximately 10:45 a.m. that day.

The President of South Vietnam Duong Van Minh, who had taken office just two days earlier, surrendered unconditionally, displaying a white flag over the palace. South Vietnamese flags like the one my daughter drew were now lowered and replaced with North Vietnamese ones.

It was not the most joyous end to see how South Vietnamese citizens feared the change that came to their doorsteps; but I've come to learn war never has a pleasant ending and suffering is inevitable.

As spring became summer, Quang and Vinh walked the land together—side by side, boots muddy, hands behind their backs like old generals surveying the future.

They started with Quang's family paddies, which had survived the chemical rain that stripped so many other farms bare. While others struggled with poisoned earth, theirs still bore green shoots. Vinh, ever the thinker, suggested combining their talents.

"You grow it," he said, tapping a stalk of rice, "and I'll sell it."

It was simple. It was brilliant. It was exactly what the village needed.

They borrowed tools, shared labor, and bought seed from a cousin up north. By harvest, they weren't just feeding our families—they were selling to neighboring villages, then towns.

Months later, Vinh pulled me aside and placed two old, weathered deeds in my hand. I unfolded it slowly, breath catching.

The first, was my mother's lands. The land where my father, mother, and brother were buried.

The second, Uncle Po's rubber grove.

"We bought them back," he said softly. "It's yours again."

I clutched the papers like they might disappear. The grove and lands our family lost. It was back in my hands.

I looked at Vinh and didn't speak. But my eyes softened. I already forgave him after his son saved mine, but this was more than I could have asked for.

Then a second gift, Vinh and Quang both held out a box to Mai and I. Our eyes igniting with flames as we peeled off the ribbon wrapping the small box. Both of us received diamond rings.

Quang and Vinh explained, "Wedding rings, we thought it was only right, now that we had enough money to make sure our wives weren't walking around with single men noticing them without a ring on their fingers."

Mai blushed her face as red as the day Vinh first said hello to us in the market. My palm sweaty as I slid the ring over my finger.

Both of us beyond content. We both knew we had amazing men.

By the end of 1980, we were the largest producers of rice and rubber in the region.

The groves flourished. The paddies gleamed. The war had taken so much, but it hadn't taken everything.

The villagers began to smile again—real smiles, not the cautious, haunted ones of survival. Children returned to school. Markets brimmed with life. The sound of hammering came not from bunkers or barricades, but from new homes being built.

And through it all, Mai and I walked the village paths together, our grandchildren in tow, watching the land grow back leaf by leaf.

The forest had scars. The rivers still whispered of pain. But there was food on the table. Laughter in the air. And a place to plant hope.

THE ONES WHO REMAIN

Summer of 1985

Years passed, and our days of hardship faded into memory, softened by time like old photographs worn at the edges.

Not everyone was as lucky as my family and Mai's. So many bore scars we couldn't see. Children were born with deformities, their tiny bodies broken by something they'd never touched: Agent Orange. It had blanketed huge parts of the country, poisoning the fields and the waters people drank. Entire generations, suffered. Many disabled people were left with what was known as the "Five Nothings," no home, no family to claim them, no ability to bear children, no prospects for marriage, and no professional or social standing.

Our own land, by some miracle, had been spared. Planes passed overhead but rarely dropped the chemical around us since American troops were stationed in the city nearby. My children and grandchildren spared of the diseases that followed. But we still saw the devastation. At the market, we'd pass mother after mother cradling babies with twisted spines, missing limbs, deformed. So many, too many children with spina bifida, bladder cancer, or leukemia, all dying before they could grow.

I remember standing beside Mai as we watched them. Her eyes filled with tears, and I felt the same helplessness deep in my chest.

We couldn't undo the war. But we could do something.

Mai asked Vinh and I asked my husband, and together we opened a shop—one where we could hire those children. Many of which were orphans, and overlooked by the world. Without hesitation, Mai and I poured everything we had into it, and together, we built something beautiful.

Using crushed eggshells and lacquer, we taught them to create traditional Vietnamese paintings—delicate, shimmering works of art. The eggshells had to be cleaned, dried, and placed with care. Every piece took patience. Time. Steady hands and open hearts. Just like healing.

Lan would visit often during her studies and help the children at our shop. She was always great with kids, using what she learned in school during her pursuit to teach.

We ran that store for many years, until age crept into our joints and slowed our steps. When it became too much, we knew who to entrust the shop to, and we passed it on to Hein and Lan. Knowing it would be safe in their hands.

Now, most mornings I sit on the porch wrapped in quiet, my hands curled around a warm cup of tea. The sun rises over the fields just like it always did—but the air is different now. No distant rumbles of war. No shouting. No rush to hide the children.

Just peace. Honest, enduring peace.

I no longer need to wake early to tend the fields with Quang. I look down at my hands—calloused, weathered—and see all the life we have built.

Quang passed on one warm autumn morning, surrounded by family. His sons held his hands. Lan wept quietly beside him. His final moments were gentle, the way he lived—smiling up at me, whispering his love for me, asking only that I keep living, keep smiling, and keep holding Mai's hand through whatever came next. He was only 63 and far too young.

He was buried on the hill overlooking the rice paddies, beside the rubber grove we reclaimed. I sat by his grave every Sunday, telling him stories of the grandchildren's antics and how tall the rice stalks had grown.

Not long after, Vinh too passed peacefully, leaving behind a legacy not of war or politics—but of love, redemption, and the quiet courage it took to right a terrible wrong. Mai held his hand to the very end, and after the funeral, she and I sat in silence together for hours, hands clasped, tears dried on our cheeks, eyes fixed on the horizon.

Our children—grown now—lived in the big cities, raising families of their own. Some became doctors, others teachers. A few moved abroad. But every Tet holiday, they came home to the village with their children in tow, bearing candies and flowers and stories from faraway places.

Mai and I, hair now silver and soft as river mist, would sneak sweets into our grandchildren's hands when their parents weren't looking—just like my *bà ngoại* used to do for me.

We walked the same dirt paths we once ran as girls, laughing over old jokes, remembering dances under the moon, and holding tight to the knowledge that we had survived the worst and still found our way back to joy.

We were the ones who remained—not because we were unscarred, but because we chose to stay, to rebuild, and to believe in love again.

As the river flowed quietly beside the village, carrying away the years, I looked over at my oldest friend and whispered, "We made it, didn't we?"

Mai smiled, eyes glistening. "We did."

And together, we watched the sun rise one more time.

The End.

Hung and Lianne never left the prison.

Six months after Mai fled south with her children, word reached the village. A cousin of Vinh's who had stayed behind confirmed it in a single, scrawled letter: "They were made examples of. Hung was paraded before the marketplace, then executed in silence. Lianne was never seen again. It is assumed she died in the women's camp."

Mai never spoke of it directly. But on nights when the wind howled across the paddies, Minh would find her sitting at the edge of the porch, eyes fixed on a distant point in the dark, hands clenched tightly in her lap.

In the mid-1990s, long after the country began healing its wounds, a letter arrived addressed to Mai. It was official, bearing the seal of a regional office. Inside was an apology. A formal statement of regret for the wrongful imprisonment of her parents. Their names, it read, had been added to a commemorative statue in a public park near the house she and Vinh once owned in the city. Mai wept as she read the names etched in bronze, even if only in a photograph.

Aunt Tam and Uncle Po never reached the South.

They vanished somewhere between the Annamite mountains and the Mekong River. Nguyet, their daughter, survived. It was years before a letter reached Minh's hands, smuggled through a merchant. Nguyet was alive, living near Can Tho with her husband Long and her son, Duy. Her voice was timid but kind in the letter, and it carried something else, too—a longing for the roots she'd lost.

Minh replied with trembling hands.

Months later, Duy arrived.

He was tall, soft-spoken, and wide-eyed, carrying the nervousness of a boy raised on stories he couldn't quite believe. He met his cousins for the first time beneath the tamarind tree, where his mother had once danced in childhood. They played cards, passed food around the table, and laughed. The bond was instant.

Beni had found his own voice. He had always followed Kiet, the comedian of our youth. But with Kiet gone and laughter scarce, Beni turned toward the stage in his own way. He moved to France, where thousands of refugees were learning to live again. There, he became a night show host—bold, loud, and full of charm. His show, "Paris by Night," was a mix of music, comedy, and traditional Vietnamese performances. He always opened the show with the same line: "Tonight, let's sing, and dance, and laugh in honor of those who never got the chance."

And every time he said it, I thought of Kiet.

Minh's daughter, Lan, had grown into a graceful, sharp-witted young woman. She taught literature at the local school and ran the Vietnamese lacquer painting shop Mai and Minh created. Hein, ever faithful to Lan, ran their fathers' rice business, managing the books, overseeing the shipments, and still made time to walk Lan home. And when the time came, he reopened his father's furniture store, and continued to share his craft with the world.

Minh's eldest son, Cuu, studied law in the capital. He returned often, full of ideas, always listening more than he spoke. He opened a modest practice, advocating land disputes and family protections in a country still stitching itself together. Her youngest, Thanh, went on to become a doctor and worked at a renowned hospital in Saigon.

Mai's children thrived, too. Anh became a midwife. Her gentle nature and quiet confidence made her beloved in every village she visited. Tie joined a cooperative and trained as an engineer, helping rebuild roads and water systems destroyed by war.

Khang would take over Thao's father's fishing business, rising before dawn each day to mend nets and guide the small crew of boys who helped him along the coast. Thao, with her love of flowers, opened a small herbal shop for healing, at the edge of the village. She sold teas, balms, and flower tinctures made from petals she dried carefully by hand.

Each year, the families gathered.

They came by bus, bike, train, and even on foot. They cooked in giant clay pots, lit paper lanterns, and let the children play in the same creek where Mai and Minh once bathed as girls. There were sons-in-law now, daughters-in-law, children, grandchildren, and even great-grandchildren. Laughter filled the fields.

At each gathering, Minh and Mai sat side by side on the porch.

Sometimes they spoke. Other times they just watched, content in the sound of life continuing.

Between them sat a small wooden box, once gifted by Vinh, which now held their matching engraved lockets: "Not sisters by blood, but by choice."

They no longer needed to wear them as a reminder, for the words they once held so dear now lived quietly, deeply, inside them.

Stephen Wasilewski is a well-known and respected business owner in Schuylkill County who provides vocational support and career development services to students with disabilities. He is a graduate of Kutztown University and Misericordia University, where he majored in social studies education and earned a master's degree in business.

He enjoys writing, traveling, and sharing his lived experiences through educational settings. His passion for history and uncovering forgotten narratives deepened during his travels across Asia. He visited historical sites such as the Củ Chi tunnels and the Independence Museum in Ho Chi Minh City, Vietnam, as well as the War and Women's Human Rights Museum in Seoul, South Korea. There, he encountered the enduring scars of war, learning about tragedies like the My Lai massacre and the suffering of Korea's "comfort women."

The River Between Us, his debut novel, was inspired by a letter he read in Korea that honored women's strength and their ability to survive horrific and inhumane conditions during wartime. Blending historical fact with fiction, the novel tells a story of survival, sisterhood, and quiet resistance in the face of sweeping political change. Stephen believes that stories, especially those rooted in pain, can heal, connect, and inspire readers to carry their own stories forward across generations.

www.ingramcontent.com/pod-product-compliance
Lightning Source LLC
Chambersburg PA
CBHW070747160726
48004CB00001B/95